THE VENGEANCE OF THE CROWS

KYLE ALEXANDER ROMINES

HELLBENDER BOOKS

an imprint of Sunbury Press, Inc.
Mechanicsburg, PA USA

an imprint of Sunbury Press, Inc.
Mechanicsburg, PA USA

For information about special discounts for bulk purchases, please contact Sunbury Press Orders Dept. at (855) 338-8359 or orders@sunburypress.com.

To request one of our authors for speaking engagements or book signings, please contact Sunbury Press Publicity Dept. at publicity@sunburypress.com.

FIRST HELLBENDER BOOKS EDITION: May 2023

Set in Adobe Garamond | Interior design by Crystal Devine | Cover design by Damonza | Edited by Jennifer Cappello.

Publisher's Cataloging-in-Publication Data
Names: Romines, Kyle Alexander, author.
Title: The vengeance of the crows / Kyle Alexander Romines.
Description: First Trade paperback edition. | Mechanicsburg, PA : Hellbender Books, 2023.
Summary: Josh Rush wants to enjoy one final getaway with his friends before the end of high school. A spooky October camping trip in rural Appalachia sounds like the perfect opportunity to do just that. But Josh doesn't know about the bloodstains at the cabin. He doesn't know about the graves. And he definitely doesn't know about something monstrous stirring in the cave. Something that won't rest until Josh and his friends are dead . . .
Identifiers: ISBN : 978-1-62006-364-4 (softcover) | ISBN : 979-8-88819-041-8 (ePub).
Subjects: BISAC : FICTION / Thrillers / Supernatural.

Product of the United States of America
0 1 1 2 3 5 8 13 21 34 55

Continue the Enlightenment!

This novel is dedicated to my brother, Burns.

"They sacrificed their sons and their daughters to false gods. They shed innocent blood, the blood of their sons and daughters, whom they sacrificed to the idols of Canaan, and the land was desecrated by their blood."

—Psalm 106:37-38

"Greater love has no one than this: to lay down one's life for one's friends."

—John 15:13

Prologue

They were coming to kill her.

Kara fled blindly under the crescent moon. The beckoning forest ahead concealed either the promise of safety or further danger within its shadowy depths. She kept going, even as her aching legs threatened to give way. Anything was better than going back.

Footsteps sounded at her back as she neared the woods. Kara dropped to her knees and hid among the cornstalks. Her chest rose and fell rapidly with each ragged breath. Her lungs burned from the oxygen demand. The forest loomed close by, tantalizingly out of reach.

She gathered her courage and cast a glance behind her, where a figure searched for her among the rows. Kara trembled at the figure's inexorable approach. Certain the thundering sound of her racing heart would give her away, she pitched herself forward and sprinted into the woods as fast as her legs could carry her. She didn't look back.

The forest was darker than she feared. The moon's silvery glow ebbed the farther she ventured. Crows watched her from branches above. Their eyes gleamed in the night. An ominous silence fell over the woods, and Kara slowed her pace. There was no sign of anyone nearby. She was alone—for the moment.

Kara walked quietly under the trees and waited for her eyes to adjust to the light's absence. Her clothes were torn and stained. Bruises and cuts marked her skin. Tears and sweat had smeared her makeup. As she wandered through the forest, her heartbeat gradually steadied and her breaths became regular. Her only thought became finding safety.

Kara stopped dead in her tracks at the sight of the cabin. It seemed to have materialized almost out of nothing, as if it had waited to spring into existence just for her. The cabin lay at the heart of a small grove, surrounded by the much denser forest. From the look of things, it had long ago fallen into disuse. She wondered briefly how much time had passed since someone set foot inside.

A dirt trail leading away from the cabin vanished into the night. Kara debated the wisdom of following the path. Perhaps it led back to the main road, and her salvation. Before she could make up her mind, the wind lessened, and she again heard someone approaching through the brush. She darted toward the cabin in a panic, tripped over a rock, and landed just outside the front door. Her hand left a bloody print on the wooden frame as she reached for the doorknob with her other hand while praying it wasn't locked.

To her relief, the door hissed open, and a sliver of moonlight illuminated the cabin's dust-covered interior. Kara scrambled inside and pushed the door shut. Her fingers trembled on the knob, and she backed away slowly. She brushed a strand of long, black hair away from her face and listened. At first, she heard only the slight wind murmuring through the trees that encircled the cabin. Afraid to breathe, Kara hovered close to the door.

Without warning, something collided violently with the door. Surprised, Kara fell back and landed on the cold floor with a thud. She clamped a hand over her mouth and suppressed a scream as the unseen force rammed itself against the entrance a second time. The door rattled on its hinges. Kara craned her neck in search of an escape, but there was nowhere to go. She was trapped. The banging grew louder, and she was sure the door would give way any moment to reveal whatever horror lurked outside.

The noise ceased as suddenly as it began. Kara remained on the floor a few moments longer in disbelief before crawling to the wall and peering out the window in search of her unseen assailant. There was no one outside the cabin, at least as far as she could see. Kara dropped away from the window, grabbed her knees, and rocked back and forth. If she remained inside the cabin, it was only a matter of time before she was discovered.

She had to run while there was still a chance—even if the figure was just outside, waiting for her to make her escape.

After stealing one last glance outside the window, Kara climbed to her feet and pressed herself against the wall. She eased the door's lock open, fastened her quivering hand around the doorknob, and took a deep breath before flinging herself outside. She followed the path that led from the cabin. A branch struck her neck and tore her skin, but she kept running. Then her foot caught a large object on the ground, and she fell face-first into the mud.

Squinting in the darkness at what had caused her to stumble, Kara pushed herself up and brushed the leaves away. Moonlight seeping around lifeless branches gave form to a human body sprawled across the damp earth. Her first impulse was to scurry away, but as the corpse's features became clearer, she turned over the body with growing horror.

"Ethan?"

Her husband's lifeless eyes stared back at her. Kara noticed something wet and sticky on his shirt, and when she drew her hands back, they were covered in blood. She held her husband's body close, but before she could mourn, a figure stepped out from behind the trees. The knife clutched in his hand shimmered in the moonlight.

Kara tried to crawl away, but she was too slow. Her attacker grabbed her ankle with his free hand and dragged her back through the mud, even as she clawed the dirt with her hands. With one last burst of strength, she kicked free and stumbled to her feet. She fled deeper into the forest with no thought of direction or her location. The farther she ran, the more the forest changed around her. There were thorns everywhere. The smell was musty—almost ancient. At last, the light became a distant memory.

Voices whispering to her in the wind made her skin crawl. Kara spun around, bracing herself, but there was no one there. Instead, she found herself face-to-face with the entrance to a cave. Despite the present threat, she hesitated. Darkness radiated from the cave. Something evil dwelled there—she was sure of it. Footsteps sounded again behind her. Left with no other recourse, Kara wandered into the cave, which seemed to grow around her and threatened to swallow her whole.

Like a hundred voices buried under the earth, the whispers, interspersed with one larger presence, rang out again, and Kara was filled with the unmistakable sensation that she was not alone.

"Hello? Is someone there?"

The whispers stopped, and a hush fell over the cave. Then her hand brushed against something feathery—something that moved. Kara jerked her hand away as a dim red light emanated from the cavern's recesses to highlight hundreds of crows lining the cavern's walls. The birds' gazes were fixed solely on her.

Her heart pounded so hard she thought it would burst. She backed away, and the crows rose as one. Before she could run, the swarm descended on her.

A shriek rang out from the cave, and there was silence once more.

Five Years Later

Chapter ONE

Josh watched the mountains passing by while keeping one eye on the road. There was something raw and majestic about the rugged Appalachian terrain, but that didn't make the steep, winding eastern Kentucky roads any less dangerous. Still, he couldn't resist the urge to take an occasional peek at the expansive world outside his window. This was the kind of thing he lived for. Josh could spend entire days trekking through nature or exploring the countryside behind the wheel. It was one of the only times he felt truly at peace.

He glanced over at his brother, Nick, in the passenger seat. They had said barely more than two words to each other since leaving Louisville. That was almost three hours ago now. Nick's last-minute addition to the group was a private source of frustration for Josh, who had planned on a small, intimate gathering of friends. Then Nick had invited himself. Josh wondered why his brother wanted to tag along in the first place. True, they had been close once, but that was years ago, before Nick left for college. Now they were practically strangers.

Josh's gaze fell on Nick's cross necklace, and his mouth folded into a frown. *That* was new. It certainly wasn't something he would have associated with his brother. When Nick noticed him staring, Josh hastily averted his eyes and tried turning on the radio to break the uncomfortable silence. He only succeeded in filling the car with static.

Nick finally ended the lull in conversation. "We're too far out for a signal."

As if he'd somehow won an unspoken contest of wills, Josh fought the urge to grin. He switched off the radio and retrieved his cell phone from the cup holder. "No bars. Guess we won't be getting any reception out here."

"I hope the others will be able to find this place."

I hope I'll *be able to find this place.* "Me too. Otherwise, we'll go hungry. They're bringing the snacks in the van."

Josh dropped the phone back into the cup holder. Without network service, his GPS app was useless. The car passed farm after farm without a soul in sight. They hadn't met another vehicle on the road in miles, not since the tractor they'd been stuck behind for a solid fifteen minutes outside Jackson County. Coupled with the towering mountains and sprawling hills, there was something dreadfully lonely about the area, even with his brother beside him.

Suddenly, his eyes went wide. Josh swore and stomped on the brake to bring the car to a screeching halt.

Nick sat straight up. "What is it?"

"I think that was our turn." Josh peered into his rearview mirror at a nearly invisible gravel trail that led into the forest. The signpost jutting out from the ground was old and faded. Its letters were no longer legible. After checking to make sure the main road was still abandoned, Josh turned the car around and veered onto the gravel path.

A deer wandering across the trail stopped and looked up at them for a moment before bounding away.

Nick watched the deer until it disappeared from view. "It's a good thing you slowed down back there. Hitting that buck would have really started our trip off on the wrong foot."

"*Our* trip?" Josh retorted.

Nick winced but didn't take the bait.

Josh maintained a steady pace the rest of the way. Kicked-up pieces of gravel pattered on the undercarriage as the low-riding car jostled over the road until they came to a bend where a dirt trail replaced the gravel.

"Are you sure this is the right way?" Nick took in the forest spread around them. There were no buildings or signs to indicate the direction they were headed.

"We'll find out." Josh remained intent on following the trail to its end. Nick slumped back in his seat with a wistful expression on his face. After several minutes spent in renewed silence, the cabin appeared at the end of the road, and Josh breathed a relieved sigh. "We're here."

It really *was* in the middle of nowhere, the perfect place for a camping trip with his friends. Josh didn't want to admit it, but the trip would probably be their last getaway together. Next week, it would be back to school and the various extracurricular activities that took up so much of his time these days. Soon it would be winter. As always, the prospect of college hung heavy on the horizon. He was lucky the fall break afforded them the opportunity, even if he was disappointed a few of his friends hadn't been able to make it. As things stood, he was really only looking forward to spending time with two of the four others, and his brother was, sadly, not included in that number.

Nick nodded at the cabin. "Wow."

Wow is right. Josh had camped in three-story luxury cabins in Gatlinburg, and he had camped in a tent on hard, unforgiving ground, but he had never seen a cabin quite like the one in front of him.

It was old—very old. That much was evident just from its appearance. He doubted the cabin had ever been painted. If it had, the paint had long ago worn away. The wood and stone exterior was weathered by time. The boards had a lifeless gray tint. Vines and weeds crept along the cabin's sides. Accumulated dry leaves spilled over the slanted roof. Given its modest size, Josh doubted there would be enough space for everyone to have their own room. It was a miracle the thing was still standing. No wonder it had been affordable on his high-school budget.

Josh parked the car in the shade under sleeping trees, where autumn leaves fluttered down onto the windshield in the faint breeze. The brothers exited the vehicle at the same time and walked to the trunk to retrieve their supplies.

Nick glanced over his shoulder. "The site looks abandoned."

Josh took a moment to survey the campsite and found himself in agreement. The lonely cabin was encircled by a wide patch of bare earth, as if the forest feared to encroach past the border of the neighboring trees. Dry, brown grass grew in scattered patches. A group of stumps surrounding a ring of stones piled in the dirt formed what once served as a fire pit. Stacked logs, moldy and rotten from neglect, rested a few feet from a rusty axe buried in a tree stump.

"How did you find out about this place?" Nick didn't endeavor to hide his skepticism.

Josh waited for him to grab his bag from the trunk and slammed it shut. The loud sound echoed through the quiet woods.

"My friend's parents own it. I don't think they get out here much."

Nick swung his bag over his shoulder. At twenty-two, he was a full four years older than Josh, who had only recently turned eighteen. Nick was a little shorter than average, but he made up for it with a boyish attractiveness Josh had always envied. In contrast, Josh, well over six feet, loomed above most of his friends and classmates. Where Nick was athletic and coordinated, Josh felt awkward and gangly. He wore his muddy brown hair long and shaggy to distract from a face he had always found too chubby and round compared to his thin frame.

Josh started toward the cabin and left Nick to catch up to him.

"Do you think your friends will be here soon?"

Josh shrugged.

Nick closed the distance between them and blocked Josh's path forward. "Is something wrong?"

Josh stopped and looked his brother in the eye. "Level with me, Nick—why did you really want to come here?"

Nick bit his lip. In the past, he might have responded with a sarcastic remark or a quick joke, part of a roguish charm Josh had always admired about his brother. Instead, there was a new weariness behind his gaze.

"I wanted to spend some time with you, that's all. We're brothers."

The vulnerability in Nick's voice irritated Josh. He didn't have the right—not after all this time.

"You left me there, alone." Fighting back growing anger, Josh dropped his bag and took a step closer to his brother. "Now you think you can pretend like everything is just like it was? I was the only one there for Mom." His gaze darkened. "You didn't even come to the funeral."

Nick's eyes fell on the faded scar that ran from Josh's mouth to his chin. "I've changed."

"People don't change, Nick."

"Who made you the authority on people?" There it was—a hint of that old personality, buried just beneath the surface. "That's a pretty high horse you're sitting on for a teenager."

"Mom used to think Dad would change, or maybe you forgot about that after you ran away to college."

"That's not fair. I haven't forgotten a thing."

"You weren't there when he . . ." Josh stopped, and they regarded each other for a long moment. "And now you wear that thing around your neck and claim you've changed, but I know who you are—who you *really* are."

He picked up his bag and stalked past his brother toward the cabin. Nick lingered behind with his head bowed. Josh hoped the others would arrive soon. He hadn't planned this trip to fix his unresolved problems with his brother, though from the look of things, that was exactly what Nick had in mind.

He was so caught up in his thoughts that he almost didn't notice the door. Josh stopped suddenly, and his brow furrowed in surprise.

"What is it?"

Josh didn't answer. He stared, unblinking, at the entrance to the cabin as Nick followed his gaze.

There, on the front door, faded by time, was the unmistakable outline of a bloody handprint.

Chapter TWO

They were lost. Brooke was sure of it, even if no one else noticed. Disregarded by the van's other occupants, she sat quietly in the back. Chad, the driver, was thoroughly distracted by the musical selections streaming from his phone through the aux cable. Reagan, Chad's girlfriend, kicked back in the passenger seat with her feet pressed against the windshield.

"I think we missed a turn somewhere." Brooke looked over her shoulder at the stretch of road behind them. "We should have been there by now."

Most likely on account of the blaring metal music vibrating the windows, neither heard her. When Brooke leaned forward, raised her voice, and tried again, Reagan shifted uncomfortably and acquired a distasteful expression.

Chad eased down the volume. "What's that?"

Brooke finally managed to make herself heard. "I think maybe we're lost."

Chad scoffed at the suggestion, but the moment he glanced away from his phone to the GPS, he unleashed a string of expletives.

"What is it?" Reagan made a show of absently checking her own phone for messages when in truth they hadn't had service for miles.

"We're off the grid." Chad tapped the GPS unit mounted above the dashboard. A series of question marks had replaced the purple highlighted route on the screen. "One of you needs to try calling Josh."

"Unless either of you have bars on your phones, I doubt that will work." Brooke did her best to keep her tone neutral. "There's no reception out here."

The others glanced again at their phones and shook their heads simultaneously.

Chad fiddled with the e-cigarette clutched between his fingers. "What now?"

"We could pull over somewhere and ask for directions," Brooke suggested.

Chad and Reagan exchanged a look. "What, go ask the hillbillies for directions?" Chad laughed. "No thanks."

Brooke shrugged. "I'm sure the people here are nice. Besides, what do we have to lose?"

Chad turned to Reagan, once again wearing her trademark patronizing smirk, for advice.

"It's worth a shot."

Chad groaned. "Fine, but if any toothless hicks try to eat us, you're on your own."

Brooke retreated to the relative seclusion of her place in the backseat. If she'd had her way, she would have ridden with Josh and Nick. Chad and Reagan were Josh's friends, not hers, though that was probably an overstatement. *Reagan* was Josh's friend. Brooke suspected Josh only put up with Chad because of her. According to Josh, Chad had lately begun insisting on joining him and Reagan whenever they spent time together. That smacked of jealousy to Brooke, but as she pictured Josh and Reagan together, it was a sentiment she understood all too well.

Chad, puffing on his e-cigarette, rolled down the window to enjoy the breeze.

"Hey!" Reagan's brow furrowed with sudden anger. "Roll that window up. The wind is messing up my hair."

Brooke interrupted the lovers' quarrel. "There's a farm ahead."

A hush fell over the vehicle. Unlike the small and modest farms sprinkled throughout the Appalachian hills, the compound Brooke pointed out was an impressive size. There were no collapsed barns or rotting fences. Instead, the rustic-looking farm appeared fully operational. A freshly painted black rail fence enclosed the property. Cornfields stretched on either side of the gravel road leading to the farmhouse.

"Why on earth would anyone want to live out here? I bet they get their water from a well." Chad turned the wheel, and the van swerved onto the gravel road. "Time to ask Jim Bob if he knows where we can find the cabin."

It wasn't clear if Chad's show of contempt was genuine or for Reagan's benefit. In Brooke's experience, Reagan disapproved of just about everything. The distant farmhouse grew in size at their approach. Brooke counted two large, painted barns, a grain silo, a tool shed, and a stone well.

"That's odd." For a moment, surprise replaced the edge of condescension in Reagan's voice. "It's October, but the corn is still green. The fields should have withered away by now."

Brooke considered the remark. She didn't doubt that Reagan knew what she was talking about. Whatever her flaws, Reagan was one of the smartest people she had ever met. That was probably one of the reasons Reagan and Josh connected the way they did. Although Brooke did reasonably well in school, those two operated on an entirely different level. She couldn't compete with their far-ranging philosophical debates or heated conversations about literary analysis.

"Who cares about the corn, babe?" Chad returned his e-cigarette to his letterman jacket. "It's probably genetically engineered or some crap like that."

"That's not how genetic engineering works." Reagan folded her arms across her chest. "Idiot."

Judging from the way Chad took such a cutting remark in stride, Brooke wondered if this was normal for their relationship.

The farmhouse loomed at the end of the road. It was every bit the picturesque country home. It was painted a cozy white, aside from black roofing and dark-tinted windows. Two rocking chairs sat empty on the front porch. Leaving a lingering trail of dust, Chad pulled up to the front of the house and put the van in park.

"Do you see anyone?" Reagan sat up straight in her seat.

Chad shook his head. "The place looks deserted."

Brooke's gaze remained fixed on the endless rows of cornstalks. "Maybe we should go." Although she had been the one to convince them to ask for directions, she suddenly had a bad feeling in the pit of her stomach.

"No way. We've come all this way—we might as well look around." Chad pulled the keys from the ignition and pushed open the door before she could say another word. Reagan followed, and Brooke reluctantly did the same.

The wind lessened, and the evening grew eerily quiet. Brooke glanced around. She wondered how many people lived in such a place. Given the size of the farm, it probably took a lot of work to keep it running. More than anything, it seemed out of place in rural Appalachia, as if hidden from the world on purpose.

Stop it. You're working yourself up over nothing.

Her eyes fell on the tool shed, where a trail of footprints was visible in the dirt. She advanced toward the spot and was just about to put her hand on the door when a gentle braying sound rang out nearby. When Brooke turned around, she spotted a goat tethered outside the closest barn.

"Hey there, little fellow." She knelt down to pet the goat's head. "Aren't you a cutie? You wouldn't happen to know where your owners are, would you?"

Chad and Reagan, over by the silo, appeared locked in another argument. Brooke studied the couple. Chad was roughly five foot ten, with a muscular, athletic body and curly blond hair. As suggested by his letterman jacket, he was one of the varsity football captains, perhaps one reason for his overconfident disposition.

Brooke cleared her throat, and the bickering ceased abruptly. "There's no one over here."

Reagan's eyes widened as she stared past her. Brooke looked at her quizzically, but before she could open her mouth, she heard a growling sound behind her. Brooke, paralyzed by fear, froze in place. A short distance away, a massive German shepherd bared a set of salivating fangs while straining at its chain to get to her. Her pulse racing wildly, Brooke stumbled away from the barn with the dog's barks breaking the silence.

"That's a guard dog if I ever saw one." Chad, perhaps intent on show-ing off, drew closer to the dog than necessary. "It's a good thing he's tied up, or you would have been his next meal."

"That's not funny." Brooke remained unable to tear her eyes away from the ferocious creature.

Reagan, on the other hand, ignored the dog completely. "What's that goat doing out here?"

Chad chuckled. "Well, babe, it *is* a farm."

"Look around. Aside from the dog, do you see any other animals? There aren't any horses or cattle in the fields. Don't you think that's just a little strange?"

"So what? Maybe it's just a corn farm or something. I swear, if you girls are spooked now, wait until it gets dark around the cabin. It is Halloween, after all." Chad raised his hands like claws. "Or at least it will be."

Reagan slugged him in the side, and not so playfully, either. "Cut it out."

For once, Brooke found herself in agreement with Reagan. Something didn't feel right. "Let's just go."

Chad raised an eyebrow. "Are you serious? We came all the way out here. There has to be someone on this farm who can tell us where to go." Leaving Brooke to tag along reluctantly, he and Reagan started toward the farmhouse. As much as she didn't want to enter the house, she had absolutely no desire to be left alone. The place gave her the creeps.

I bet Josh and Nick are starting to wonder where we are. She had been surprised to learn Josh's brother was tagging along. Brooke hadn't seen Nick in years. She knew that he had dropped out of college. There were rumors about substance abuse, but there had *always* been rumors about the Rush family, as far back as she could remember. Josh didn't talk much about his brother, and Brooke wasn't one to press the subject, which she sensed was a sore one for him.

Chad casually sauntered over to the screen door and pressed the doorbell several times in succession. Silence greeted them.

Reagan prevented Chad from pressing the doorbell again. "Clearly, it's out of order."

Chad creaked open the screen door and rapped loudly on the wooden frame. "Hello? Anyone there?"

Brooke tried peering through a window. The house was dark. She didn't see any sign of human inhabitants.

Chad grabbed the doorknob.

Brooke put a hand over his forearm. "Wait. Maybe we shouldn't. Isn't this breaking and entering?"

Chad gestured to the abandoned farmland. "Do you see anyone else around here?" He twisted the doorknob, and the door screeched open. "Come on, I want to see what it looks like inside." With that, he pushed the door aside and crossed the threshold, and Reagan entered behind him. Brooke cast a furtive glance behind her and reluctantly followed them inside.

Natural light crept inside the farmhouse through the single-pane windows. Brooke wandered into the parlor, where two candles on end tables cast their dim light across the room. Despite the candlelight, shadows lurked in every corner. Brooke felt as if the house had been waiting—waiting for her.

"There are no pictures," Reagan muttered. She was right. As Brooke's gaze swept over the room, she didn't see any keepsakes that might suggest this was someone's home.

Chad's voice bellowed from the next room. "Hello!"

Brooke quickened her pace. Finding herself separated from the others in such a place was the last thing she wanted.

Chad had found his way into the kitchen. "Where do you think everyone is?" The grin on his face faltered enough to expose a crack in his self-assured demeanor.

Before Brooke could answer, a bony hand grabbed her from behind. "What are you doing here?"

Brooke turned around and found herself face-to-face with an old woman with deep-set eyes and a hooked nose. She was roughly Brooke's height—five foot four—and wore a plain gray dress. Her gray and white hair was arranged in a long braid, and wrinkles lined her face.

The woman leaned closer toward her. "Well?"

Taken aback by the woman's sudden appearance, Brooke was at a loss for words.

Chad spoke up before she could find her voice. "Sorry. We didn't mean to intrude."

"And yet you decided to enter, uninvited." The woman watched them with an inscrutable expression that made Brooke feel as if she were being dissected.

"My inarticulate boyfriend meant to say we're lost." Reagan put on a false smile. "We were looking for someone who could give us directions before we ran out of gas. It was wrong to come inside without permission, but we were too worried to think straight."

Brooke couldn't believe it. If she didn't know the tank was full of gas, she might have bought the lie herself. Reagan could bend the truth effortlessly when she bothered to turn on the charm.

The woman's frown curled into a smile. "Why didn't you say so?" She ushered them back through the parlor. "Where are you headed?"

Brooke remained uneasy at how quickly the woman's mood had changed. She couldn't shake the feeling that had bothered her before.

"There's supposed to be a cabin nearby." Chad, apparently, didn't share her concern. "Our friends are waiting for us, but we don't have reception out here."

Brooke wished he hadn't been so quick to divulge the information.

"I think I know just the place." Once they reached the front door, the old woman pointed to the forest. "You barely missed the turn. It's back that way. The path is visible from the woods. There's a sign, but the lettering is faded. It's easy to miss if you don't know what you're looking for."

"Thank you." Brooke was grateful the old woman wasn't angrier about their intrusion.

"You're welcome to stay longer if you like. I was just making some tea."

"We should probably be leaving." Reagan bit her lip. Was she suspicious too? "We want to get there before the sun sets."

"As you wish." The woman called after them as they turned to go. "By the way, how long are you planning on staying in these woods?"

"Just a couple of days." Chad threw open the van door.

"In that case, Happy Halloween."

As they pulled back onto the road, Brooke noticed the old woman watching them from the porch. Her smile was gone.

Chapter THREE

Nick's eyes lingered on the bloody handprint. It was unmistakably human. He wondered to whom it had belonged. The sight troubled him, even if it appeared not to have had the same effect on Josh, who had already entered the cabin.

"Are you coming or not?"

Nick cast a final glance at the print and crossed the threshold into the cabin, where a musty smell immediately struck him. He waved his hand in a vain attempt to dispel the heavy scent. Wooden floorboards groaned under his feet.

The cabin was larger than it appeared from the outside. A spacious open hall included an empty, blackened fireplace and a few spartan pieces of furniture. Mounted deer heads adorned the wall near a modest adjoining kitchen and two small bedrooms.

Nick stepped over a soiled rug. "How long do you think it's been since anyone's been inside?" There were cobwebs and dust everywhere. He watched a roach crawl across the rug and disappear into a crack in the wall.

"Probably years."

Nick noted the absence of any switches or electric outlets. "No lights." Indoor plumbing was probably out of the question, as none of the rooms had a toilet.

"Don't worry. I came prepared." Josh fished through his bags and pulled out a battery-powered lantern, which he set on a table before proceeding to dump a collection of flashlights beside it. "There's a flashlight for everyone in case we decide to go adventuring."

Nick fought the impulse to smile. Some things never changed. Josh might be taller now, and there was definitely more hair on his face, but deep down he was the same kid who used to love exploring sinkholes and abandoned houses. It was a reminder of better days.

Josh has every right to be angry with me. Lord knows I deserve it.

Josh's rejection hurt all the same. When they were younger, his brother looked at him with eyes full of enthusiastic admiration. Nick had hoped the trip would give him the opportunity to reconcile with his younger brother, but the impending arrival of Josh's friends presented an obstacle to his intentions.

"All you can do is try," Grace had told him, and Nick knew she was right. She always was.

He brushed a cobweb aside and walked into the kitchen. Ancient-looking china sat in dusty glass-paneled cabinets. Wooden bowls and cast-iron utensils lay idle in the drawers and shelves. Some dark-tinted jars looked as if they hadn't been opened in fifty years. The flimsy kitchen table threatened to collapse at the slightest provocation. There was nothing in the way of food, not that he had expected to find any.

"What are we doing for rooming arrangements?" Nick inspected the bedrooms. The mattresses, almost as stiff as the floor, were old and yellow.

"Brooke will get her own room. Reagan and Chad will share the other. That leaves the floor for you and me."

"Beats sleeping outside, I guess. Does anyone else live out here?" Nick thought again of the bloody handprint.

"I don't think so. There might be a farm or two within a few miles, but we should be alone for the next couple of days."

The sound of tires approached before Nick could respond. The sun had already started to set outside the cabin. Josh stopped rifling through his things and hurried out the door to greet his friends. Nick, more reserved, trailed behind. He hadn't spent a lot of time with Josh's friends. Of the rest of the group, he only knew Brooke, and that was from years ago.

The van pulled up beside Josh's car, already covered in multicolored leaves. Josh seemed to be looking for someone in particular. As the van doors opened, Nick watched Josh's gaze fall on the young woman exiting the passenger side.

Reagan, he guessed.

The look in Josh's eyes was unmistakable. He was clearly smitten with her, probably head over heels. It wasn't hard to see why. Reagan was stunning. She had a set of captivating green eyes and flawless fair skin. Her shoulder-length auburn hair shone like a burning flame. She was a little on the short side, but from the way Josh's eyes moved over her slender figure, their considerable height difference wasn't a problem. Despite her beauty, something about her struck Nick as cold, even at first glance.

Reagan noticed him regarding her. Their eyes met for a moment before her attention fell on his cross necklace, and her lips pulled back in a smirk.

"Hi, Nick," Brooke greeted him warmly, and Nick averted his gaze from Reagan. "It's good to see you again. How have you been?"

"Good. And yourself?"

Brooke shrugged. "I'm ready for school to be over."

"I remember what that's like." Nick had spent much of his high school career dreaming of leaving home and never looking back, which eventually he did.

Brooke came over to hug him, and Nick found himself touched by the gesture. Whatever stories she might have heard about him, Brooke was still the same kind girl who used to pal around with Josh when they were kids.

"What happened?" Josh approached the others. "I thought you'd get here before now."

"Next time, pick a place with reception," Reagan said matter-of-factly, holding up her phone. "Now I'm stuck with no service in the middle of the boonies."

Brooke practically rushed over to Josh. "We missed the turn." She ran a hand through her brown hair. "We stopped at the creepiest farm down the road to ask for directions."

Even as a child, Brooke had a huge crush on Josh, and from the way she looked at him now, it was clear she still felt the same way.

Neither of them is with the person they want, it dawned on Nick as the final member of the group swaggered out of the car while smoking an electronic cigarette.

"Don't tell me this is the place." The stranger, who wore a letterman jacket, threw his arm around Reagan's shoulders.

"Afraid so." Josh smiled politely at him, but Nick noticed a hint of dislike concealed in his expression.

"I'm Chad." Chad extended a hand to Nick by way of introduction, but when Nick reached for it, he jerked it back with a laugh. "You're going to have to be faster than that, bro."

Reagan slipped free of Chad's grasp. Disappointment was written on her face. "What's there to do around here?"

"This place is great." Josh somehow managed to summon up enough enthusiasm for the rest. "There's supposed to be a lot of old stuff lying around, and I think there's a fishing pond somewhere nearby."

"Hear that, babe?" Chad aimed a wink at Reagan. "We can go skinny-dipping."

Josh spoke through clenched teeth. "Let's get everything stashed inside before dark, and I'll start a campfire outside."

Chad opened the back of the van, and everyone gathered their various supplies and hauled them to the cabin.

"There are only two bedrooms." Josh hoisted a bag over his shoulder. "I figured—"

Chad reached for Reagan's rear end. "You're going to keep me warm tonight, right, babe? You know what they say about those cold October nights."

Josh looked crestfallen at the sight of them together. As the couple walked hand-in-hand toward the cabin, Nick noticed Reagan casting a furtive glance at Josh that conveyed some hidden meaning known only to them.

What did I get myself into?

With the sun gone, dusk descended over the woods. It was already dark by the time Josh got the fire going. All their belongings and supplies had been tucked safely away inside the cabin. Nick loitered at the edge of the trees and listened to the sounds coming from within the forest while the flames crackled to life behind him. A seemingly abnormal number of crows lining the branches of the trees looked back at him.

The full moon cast its cold glow over the campsite. The light, blotted out by the towering trees, vanished deeper in the woods. Nick turned back to the fire pit, where Josh sharpened sticks with a pocketknife for his friends to roast marshmallows in the flames. Surprised his brother still had the knife, which he had given him as a gift years ago, Nick walked over to the group and took a seat on an empty stump beside Brooke.

"Want a s'more?" She delicately balanced a marshmallow and a piece of chocolate over a graham cracker.

"Thanks." Nick savored the sweet dessert. Suddenly thirsty, he nodded to Chad, closest to the cooler. "Throw me some water, will you?"

Chad downed his third can and tossed it away. "How about a beer?" Nick shook his head. "What are the odds? You're the only one here actually old enough to drink, and you haven't had a single beer."

Josh reached over Chad, grabbed a water bottle, and tossed it to Nick. He also wasn't drinking, and neither was Brooke. Reagan was still nursing her first beer, but Chad was already tearing his way through the case.

Brooke, perhaps hoping to change the subject, smiled at him. "I like your necklace." Across from them, Reagan laughed at something Josh said and playfully touched his arm, and Brooke's smile slipped a bit. "Where did you get it?"

"It belonged to someone I knew." Nick, aware Josh was listening, cradled the cross in his fingers.

Like a child caught with his hand in the cookie jar, Josh cleared his throat and stood up. "I want to thank each of you for being here tonight. It means a lot to me. With college coming up next year, I wanted one last chance for us to get together. I know everyone couldn't make it, but I'm glad you're all here." His gaze lingered on Nick for a moment, as if to say, *Except for you.*

Chad shook his head. "All you and Reagan ever talk about is college. I'm sitting on a football scholarship, and you don't see me going on about it."

Reagan frowned at her boyfriend. "The Ivy League is a different thing altogether. Josh got a thirty-six on his ACT. That's a perfect score. He can go anywhere he wants." She looked at Josh admiringly, and even in the dimness, Nick could see him blush.

Chad took a swig of beer and cast yet another empty can aside. "All I'm saying is, y'all are so smart, but what do you have to show for all that work? I've never studied a day in my life, and I'm the one who'll end up with the full-ride and the girl." He pulled an uncomfortable-looking Reagan toward him and reached for another beer. "You know what the problem is with guys like you? You just don't have that killer instinct."

"Chad," Reagan whispered as he continued to hold her close.

Chad winked at Josh. "Then again, look who I'm talking to."

No one made a sound until Chad popped the tab.

It was Nick who broke the silence. "Chad, I think maybe you've had enough."

Chad snickered and held up the beer. "What, this? The party's just getting started, bro!"

Josh cast Nick a look as if to say, *I don't need your help.*

"I still don't get it." Brooke again made an obvious attempt to steer the conversation away from near-disastrous territory. "Why this place? I mean, it's definitely a change of scenery, but there are plenty of nicer campgrounds a lot closer to home."

Nick had wondered the same thing. Although each of the campers came from Kentucky, they were all from the city. Louisville's dense, urban environment was a far cry from the farms and small towns scattered across the state.

"I'm glad you asked that, Brooke." Josh's anger at Chad faded, and he grinned.

Nick knew that look all too well. *He's going somewhere with this.*

"Have any of you given any thought to *where* we are?" Josh's excitement was palpable. No one spoke up, which Nick suspected was the point. "There's a reason I picked this spot for our Halloween getaway. It's less than an hour from Gray Hollow."

Nick's brow furrowed. "The town where the tornado hit a few years back?"

Josh leaned closer to the fire and spoke slowly, as if making a solemn proclamation. "There was no tornado."

Reagan wore a bemused expression. "Not this again. More conspiracy theories?"

"It's not a conspiracy theory. It's all online. A series of murders took place just before the supposed 'tornado.' The sheriff went missing afterward, never to be seen again. I found posts on Reddit from someone who said he was there. He claimed Gray Hollow was taken over by scarecrows, and the town covered it up."

"Scarecrows? Come on, man." Chad let out a prolonged belch. "You're going to have to do better than that if you want to scare us."

"I'm not finished yet. Less than a year ago, a few people were found murdered on a farm in Booneville, not too far from here, actually. Police reports said a kid who lived on the farm was terrified of something the previous owner had locked away."

Reagan rolled her eyes. "Let me guess. It was a scarecrow."

Josh nodded.

Brooke shuddered. "Okay, now you're starting to creep me out."

Nick could tell the others remained as unconvinced as he was. "It could be a coincidence."

"That's what I thought at first." Josh retrieved a folded-up piece of paper from his pocket. "So, I dug deeper."

"What's that?" Brooke asked.

"It's a map of the state of Kentucky." Josh held the map above the firelight, and everyone leaned closer for a better look. Dozens of red circles were clustered over the eastern half of the state.

"What does it mean?" Even Reagan appeared intrigued now.

Josh looked up from the fire and waited until he had everyone's attention before continuing.

"These represent people who have gone missing over the last fifteen years. And this," he said, tapping at a place at the center of the cluster, "is where *we* are."

Chapter FOUR

No one said a word after Josh delivered his pronouncement. He stared at the others and waited for a response.

"You're such a goofball." Brooke threw a marshmallow at him across the fire. "I can't believe you dragged us all the way out here just because you read about an urban legend on some forum. That's such a 'Josh' thing to do."

Josh ducked the projectile and laughed. "What? I thought it would be the perfect way to get into the Halloween spirit. Think about it. Who knows what's in these woods?"

"You've got a morbid sense of humor. I, for one, love it." Reagan's eyes had a mischievous twinkle.

Josh found himself entranced by her gaze. The moment was cut short when Chad kissed her neck, and Josh looked away sheepishly and tried to hide his disappointment.

He used to tell himself he would never fall in love. Whatever attraction his parents once shared, it certainly hadn't been love. For most of his adolescence, Josh wasn't even sure such a thing really existed. Sure, he knew what it felt like to experience affection for his family and friends, but romantic love? Deep down, he believed it was a lie, an artifice cooked up by Hollywood and Hallmark to sell movie tickets and Valentine's cards.

That was before he met Reagan, and Josh realized that all his emphatic protestations against love were just feeble attempts to guard his heart against getting hurt. Around Reagan, he was weak and vulnerable, like he always feared he would be, and yet he didn't care. When he fell for her, he fell *hard*.

"Earth to Josh." Brooke tossed another marshmallow his way. "What are you thinking about?"

He turned away from Chad and Reagan. "Nothing."

The conversation picked up from there. They laughed about old times and spoke of their goals and aspirations for the future. It was everything Josh had hoped for and more, even if not all of his friends had been able to make it. Nick remained mostly quiet. There was clearly something he wanted to say but hadn't yet found the words for. Although Josh knew the resentment he harbored toward his brother wasn't healthy, he couldn't help the way he felt. The emotions were still too raw.

As the night dragged on and the talking dwindled, the group decided to search for the fishing pond. Given the season, the waters were undoubtedly frigid, but that was part of the lure. They were free to be immature teenagers for a while longer at least. Josh looked forward to the chance to explore the woods under the cover of night. He was a little let down that the others hadn't been impressed by his story about the scarecrows. While he was certain there was nothing supernatural about it, the reports were undeniably creepy.

He waited outside the cabin as the others went inside to retrieve towels and flashlights. Nick, lingering at the trees' edge, stared pensively into the forest. There *was* something different about him. The Nick he remembered was always the life of the party. In the past, Nick worked hard to keep up appearances, but now even his clothes were casual and nondescript.

Josh's eyes fell again on Nick's cross necklace. *They've brainwashed him.*

Brooke interrupted his musings. "Hello there."

"Back at you."

"You were doing it again—drifting off, I mean."

He nodded. "I guess there's a lot on my mind tonight."

"For all of us." Was she blushing? He couldn't tell in the firelight. "We haven't had the chance to talk yet, just the two of us. How have you been? I haven't seen a lot of you lately."

"I've been pretty busy." The words, while strictly true, still managed to convey a lie at the same time. Lately, Reagan had been taking most of his time—even from his friends and schoolwork.

Brooke laid a hand on his shoulder. "Well, I'm glad we're here now." Her hand lingered for an instant longer than necessary.

"Me too." Josh started to say something else to break the awkward silence that followed, but the others reemerged from the cabin, and his breath caught in his chest when he saw Reagan's bikini.

"Let's get this party started." She winked to show him she was well aware of the effect her appearance had on him.

"Yeah." Josh, who ordinarily prided himself on his levelheadedness, suddenly found himself at a loss for words. He turned back to Brooke, already walking away, and switched on his flashlight. "Aren't you coming with us?"

"You guys go ahead. That water will be too cold for me. I'll stay here where it's nice and warm."

"Are you sure?"

Brooke settled by the campfire and warmed her hands. "Don't worry about me. I'll have my bag of marshmallows to protect me." She tossed one in the air.

Josh tried to muster a grin, but it was a poor attempt. He couldn't help feeling guilty, like he was letting her down.

They had known each other since they were kids. They had laughed together, cried together, and shared so much with each other over the years. Brooke was his best friend long before he met Reagan. Despite how much she meant to him, Josh knew she wanted more. He did love her, but like a sister.

"Come on, bro." Chad grabbed another beer can for the road. "Let's go before it gets too cold."

Josh pointed his flashlight into the woods and followed them away from the campsite. "We won't go far, Brooke. We'll be back soon."

"I'll stay here with her," Nick offered.

Josh fought the impulse to grin, and not simply because his older brother hadn't insisted on tagging along. Fewer people meant a greater likelihood that he might get some alone time with Reagan.

They set off down the path leading into the woods. Josh was glad they'd come in October. It would have been nearly impossible to navigate the forest in the heat of summer with the brush in full bloom. Even with the moon heavy above, the dense forest all but devoured the light. Josh trained his flashlight on the overgrown path, and they made their way deeper into the woods.

A short time later, they came across a place where the brush thinned to reveal a large pond in the pines' shade, where black waters shimmered under the moonlight. Chad dropped his towel, chucked the beer can, and ran at the water, shouting like a madman. Before Josh could blink, he'd disappeared under the onyx surface.

"Come on in!" Chad resurfaced with a splash. "The water's great!"

Yeah, right. You just want us to freeze like you.

Reagan advanced toward the pond, but Josh grabbed her wrist. They stood under the trees, just out of Chad's line of sight.

Josh lowered his voice to just above a whisper. "I just wanted to talk to you."

Reagan cast a glance in the water's direction to make sure Chad wasn't looking. Then she stood on her tiptoes and kissed him on the mouth. "Not now."

The taste of her lips made his knees weak. "I'm tired of all this sneaking around. You know how I feel about you."

"Josh, we've talked about this. I like you, but you know what this is." With that, she let go of his hand and sprinted toward the pond. Josh remained where he was, watching as the dark water swallowed her moonlit body.

It wasn't simply that Reagan was beautiful, though she was to such an extent it sometimes hurt Josh to look at her. He connected with her in a way he hadn't with any girl before. She was clever and quick-witted—every bit his match. They liked the same books and shared most of the same beliefs. Their personalities meshed perfectly. Every moment they spent together, he found himself falling deeper. He was like a man possessed.

There was just one little problem, and his name was Chad. It killed Josh seeing Reagan with an infantile jock like him, but she'd made it clear from the start that she had a boyfriend and she and Josh would never be more than friends. Josh hadn't cared. He only wanted to be with her, in any capacity. Then one night, angry at Chad, Reagan reciprocated Josh's feelings, and everything became infinitely more complicated.

"So, Reagan, huh?" Nick appeared at his back. "I thought you said you'd never fall in love."

"And I thought you were going to stay at the campfire with Brooke." Josh wasn't exactly in the best mood at the moment, and he didn't need his brother making things worse.

"Speaking of Brooke, I think she's still as into you as ever."

"What are you doing here, Nick? I'm guessing you didn't come all this way to talk about my love life."

"We didn't get a chance to talk earlier. *Really* talk, I mean."

"What's there to talk about? Don't tell me you're here to convert me."

Nick looked down at the cross hanging from his neck. "It bothers you that much?"

"You were the one who told me religion was a scam, or have you forgotten that? Do you really think there's some big guy upstairs, watching everything we do?"

Nick hesitated, as if debating the matter internally. "Yeah, Josh—I do."

Josh frowned. That wasn't an answer he was ready to accept. "When we were kids, I used to pray every night that God would stop Dad from hurting us. Where was God then, Nick? If a God existed who would allow something like that to happen, He wouldn't be the kind of God I would want to worship anyway." He looked away.

Nick followed his gaze to the water. "Look, Josh, I'm not here to convert you. I'm not a theologian. I can't tell you why evil happens in the world. I only know what God's done for me."

Josh scoffed. "And what has He done for you? The last I heard, you were a college dropout with a drinking problem. That doesn't exactly sound like a redemption story to me."

"I'm working now, as an EMT. I haven't had a drink in almost a year. Listen, I know I wasn't there for you when you needed me. There are so many things I screwed up. I just . . . I just want us to be close again. We're all we have left."

Josh held his gaze and shook his head. "No. I'm all *you* have left. I have friends now, in case you haven't noticed. I don't need you anymore."

Before Nick could reply, a scream rang out from the water. The pair rushed toward the pond, where Reagan was staring at the opposite bank.

"What is it?" Josh asked. "What's the matter?"

"I'm not sure." She sounded uncharacteristically uncertain. "I thought I saw something over by the bushes."

Although he followed her gaze, he didn't spot anything out of the ordinary among the weeds and shrubs. "Like an animal?"

"Like a person."

She should have gone with the others.

Listening for her friends over the sounds of the night, Brooke sat huddled in front of the campfire. *They should have been back by now.*

She wished she had asked Nick to stay behind, or at least accompanied him to join the others. At least then she might have had some fun, instead of sulking like a stereotypical heartsick teenager while the rest of the group enjoyed themselves. She just couldn't stomach the sight of Josh drooling over Reagan in a bikini.

Why can't he see that she's wrong for him? With Reagan, everything was about herself. She didn't care about people—she only cared about what they could do *for* her. Reagan had Josh wrapped around her little finger to the point where they were sneaking around behind Chad's back. That wasn't who Josh was, not really. Josh wasn't even the only 'other guy,' at least if there was any truth to the rumors going around school. Still, it wasn't Brooke's place to tell him that. If Josh was going to see Reagan for what she was, he needed to do it on his own.

After a while, the flames sank low, and the trees' shadows crept toward the cabin. Their branches, like claws, reached for her. Brooke tossed another log onto the fire and watched it glow as the flames hungrily consuming it sent black smoke into the air. She didn't like being alone, and not only on account of Josh's unsettling story about the scarecrows. Something hadn't sat right with her since the moment they stopped for directions at that weird farm earlier, and the sinister-looking cabin hadn't improved matters.

A twig snapped somewhere in the darkness beyond the firelight.

"Hello? Is someone there?"

There was no response. Save for the stirring of the wind and the crackling of the flames, everything was quiet. Brooke, suddenly on edge, slowly stood. She couldn't shake the feeling that she wasn't alone—that she was being watched. She took a step toward the trees.

Brooke sensed movement behind her, and when she spun around, the cabin door was ajar.

"Guys?" She tried to sound brave. It was probably another one of Josh's pranks. He knew how frightened she got. Well, this time she wouldn't give him the satisfaction. Brooke grabbed a flashlight and quietly approached the cabin. Noises came from inside. As she drew nearer, the lantern inside began to flicker, and its blue glow faded. Brooke pushed the door the rest of the way open and looked around. "Hello?"

The sound went quiet. She scanned the cabin with the high-powered flashlight and searched for its source, but from what she could see, the cabin was empty. Then a hiss came from across the room, and Brooke felt gooseflesh break out on her arms. Something came running at her through the darkness. The flashlight's beam fell on a raccoon that had been digging through their food. Frightened, the raccoon darted out of the cabin.

As Brooke followed its path with the flashlight, the beam fell on the outline of something else lingering under the trees. When Brooke moved the flashlight in its direction, she saw a figure regarding her from the darkness. She screamed, lost her balance, and landed on her rear. The beam shot into the sky and was engulfed by the black expanse. When she again pointed the flashlight toward the spot where the man had been, the flashlight shaking in her hands, the space was empty. He was gone.

Josh and the others came running out of the woods before she could find her footing.

"Brooke, what is it?" Josh's brow furrowed. "What happened?"

Trembling, she stared past him into the forest. "There was someone there, watching me." She pointed to the place where the figure had stood. "It all happened so fast. I didn't get a good look at him."

Josh and Nick exchanged glances.

"What is it?"

Josh helped her up and held her by the shoulders to reassure her. "Back at the pond, Reagan thought she saw something too."

Relief flooded through her veins. She wasn't alone after all. "I was afraid you wouldn't believe me. Did you get a good look at him, Reagan?"

Everyone turned toward Reagan. There was a brief silence.

Reagan's gaze moved from Josh's hands to Brooke's shoulder, and she looked at Brooke with a cold expression. "Don't tell me you guys believed me. I was just making it up. I didn't actually see anything."

Josh broke into a huge grin. "Now I get it. You guys were trying to get me back for that story. Nice try, Brooke—you had me going there for a second."

"But I really saw someone," Brooke protested. "Honest." She looked to the others for support, but they all appeared skeptical, with the possible exception of Nick.

Reagan ran a towel over her damp hair. "Come on, Brooke." Her voice dripped with scorn. "You've had your fun. Enough pretending."

The others returned to the cabin and left Brooke, alone and very afraid, to stare into the dark.

Chapter FIVE

Sometimes he still woke up screaming.

It was the same dream every time. The fragments of memory stuck in his mind like shards of glass. Josh remembered the feel of the gun shaking in his hands. The sound of his mother's screams tore at his heart. There were flashes of his father's face, contorted in rage like some kind of feral beast. There was a deafening blast, and then . . .

Josh wiped the sleep from his eyes. Light seeped into the cabin. *What time is it?* His gaze fell on a nearby pile of blankets on the cabin floor. Nick was already gone, thank God. The last thing he wanted was for his older brother to see one of his nightmares. Josh looked around to make sure he was alone.

"Hi there, sleepyhead." Brooke held out a steaming cup of coffee from the sofa where she sat.

Josh propped himself up. "Did I . . ."

"No one heard a thing. Chad and Reagan are still asleep in their room, and your brother is outside making breakfast."

Nick, making breakfast? That was an image he couldn't reconcile in his head.

"It's so peaceful out here. I'm glad we came. My mind must have been playing tricks on me last night."

Josh, thankful the fall break afforded him the opportunity to sleep in, shook himself free of the blankets and plopped onto the sofa beside her.

"Thanks." He gratefully accepted the mug from Brooke.

"I know how you get after your beauty sleep."

There was something about her smile that had always been able to lift his spirits. He couldn't imagine Reagan making him coffee. Whatever her virtues, Reagan wasn't exactly known for her thoughtfulness. Brooke, on the other hand, usually thought about everyone else first and herself last.

"Remember that time when we were kids and we tried to make coffee?"

She nodded. "We couldn't figure out how the machine worked."

Josh chuckled, which threatened to spill the steaming coffee over the chipped mug's rim. "We made such a mess."

"My parents were so mad."

Josh took a sip. "I'm really going to miss this—us."

"I'm not going anywhere, silly."

"That's not what I meant."

Her smile faded. "I know."

College was the unspoken eventuality behind every conversation. Despite the bonds he had forged, in less than a year's time, they would all be going their separate ways, perhaps forever. The end of adolescence loomed large, with only the promise of the unknown waiting in its place. Josh was determined to enjoy every moment while it lasted.

Brooke cast a glance at the window. "He loves you, you know—your brother."

"You still haven't given up trying to solve everyone's problems, I see."

"You should give him a chance, that's all I'm saying."

Before Josh could reply, the door opened behind them, and Chad and Reagan came walking out. Reagan, wearing one of Chad's t-shirts, looked spectacular even with no makeup.

"What's that smell?" Chad sniffed the air. "I'm starving."

Josh's stomach growled in agreement, and the campers filed outside, where Nick was frying bacon and eggs over the fire pit. The group helped themselves to the bounty. Only Reagan turned down a plate when Nick offered it to her.

"No thanks. I'm vegan."

Nick didn't look very surprised by the news.

"I wouldn't mind another helping." Josh took the plate meant for her. It took a ravenous appetite to support his six-foot-four frame. He ignored an annoyed look from Reagan, who claimed eating meat tacitly endorsed cruelty to animals, one of many political causes she championed.

Brooke settled beside him. "So, what's on the agenda for this fine Halloween morning?"

Josh glanced in the direction of the distant mountains, where a patch of dark clouds lingered over fog-capped peaks. Despite the daylight, the sky was an ominous gray, hinting at the possibility of storms to come. Although the inclement weather was in keeping with the season, he hoped to avoid the rains long enough to do some exploring.

"I thought we might look around while we have the light. I've heard there are some caves in the area."

That was an understatement. Kentucky was home to the Mammoth Cave system, a sprawling underground labyrinth spanning over three hundred and ninety square miles across the state—and that was merely what had already been mapped. Technically, everything underground was government property, but in the woods, there was no one around to see.

After their late breakfast, they changed clothes inside the cabin and stocked up on supplies before beginning the trek into the woods. A short distance from the fishing pond, Josh spotted a rusted iron spike in the dirt.

"Whoa." He knelt down to retrieve it and showed it to the others. "Where do you think this came from?"

"Over here. Check it out." Chad stood on what appeared to have once been a set of railroad tracks. "There's stuff like this everywhere." He grabbed another rusted spike.

Josh guessed the rail line had probably carried coal from the mines years ago. Likely abandoned for decades, it had now crumbled from disuse. When Josh started toward the tracks, he caught a glimpse of a sign hanging from one of the neighboring trees. He approached the poster nailed into the bark. Although faded, the capital letters remained legible.

NO TRESPASSING

"Josh, I thought you said no one else lived out here." Brooke sounded worried.

Chad answered for him. "Someone probably left this here a long time ago. I bet nobody's been out here in years."

"I wouldn't be too sure about that." Nick pointed out a set of foot-prints. It appeared the tracks were fresh.

Josh recalled the bloody handprint, which he still couldn't make sense of. "People have been living in the backwoods of Kentucky for generations, since they were making moonshine during Prohibition."

"Okay, Mr. Thesaurus," Chad said caustically.

Reagan rolled her eyes. "Encyclopedia, Chad."

"Whatever. My stepdad flies a chopper, and he says there are tons of drug farms all across rural Appalachia. Just think about it—there could be a weed farm right here in these hills."

Reagan ignored the remark. "Let's see where these lead." She stepped over a barbed wire fence that had been deformed by time and rust, and the others followed suit.

Nick caught up to Josh farther down the trail. "Hey, Josh. I just wanted to apologize for last night. I've been trying to say I'm sorry—for everything."

Chad was too close behind for Josh to reply. Mindful of Brooke's advice, he let the words hang in the air. He wished things were different between him and his brother. When he was younger, he had practically worshiped the ground Nick walked on.

Their father was a drunk on his best days. On his worst . . . well, physical abuse wasn't a strong enough phrase to describe how much the family suffered at his hands. Even then, Nick always stuck up for Josh, always protected him.

"One day, I'm getting us out of here," Nick used to say.

As they aged, and their father grew increasingly unhinged, the clashes between Nick and their dad became more frequent. When Nick turned eighteen, he left home for college and never looked back, abandoning Josh and his mother to face the old man alone. Now Nick wanted to start over, but Josh wasn't sure he was ready to forgive him. Not after everything that had happened.

Ahead, Reagan had almost vanished from sight. Josh quickened his pace and pushed through the brush in an effort to keep up. Then he saw her stop dead in her tracks in a small clearing where an eerie silence hung over the forest.

"What is it?" As Josh approached, he heard flies buzzing in the stillness. Nothing grew inside the clearing. Everything was dead. The bare soil was a dark brown. From the look of things, it had been recently disturbed.

"Gross." Chad wrinkled his nose. "What's that smell?"

Josh followed Reagan's gaze to a mound of freshly piled earth not far from where a shovel stood propped against a tree. Was that blood smeared on the handle? He couldn't tell.

Hundreds of flies swarmed above the plot, which he realized was just one of many. Josh took a step back, and something brittle snapped under his shoe. When he lifted his foot, he saw a broken jawbone jutting out of the earth. The bone was one of several scattered across the clearing.

Chad picked up a rib and dangled it in front of Josh. "You're the expert. What kind of animal was it?"

Josh's blood ran cold. "Those aren't animal bones."

Chad's grin faded, and the bone slipped from his hand. "You're messing with me."

"Over here." Reagan remained fixated on the ground that had been disturbed. "Look at this."

Josh swatted away the flies. A human hand, pale and withered, stuck out of the soil.

"These are all graves. Human graves." They had stumbled onto a mass burial ground.

"Uh, guys?" Nick glanced around. "Has anyone seen Brooke?"

Chapter SIX

3:56 P.M.

She was lost—again—but unlike before, this time she was truly alone.

Brooke searched for her friends in a quiet part of the forest. She hadn't intended to lose sight of the others when she stopped to rest and take a drink. One second she'd been with the rest of the group, and the next they were gone.

"Hello!" The word, shouted at the top of her lungs, reverberated until the breeze slowly replaced it.

Keep it together. The others can't have gone far. I'll just head back to the cabin and wait until they return. The trouble was, she couldn't exactly remember where the cabin was. The overgrown path they'd started on had faded into the surrounding woods shortly after they'd set out. The dense forest was an unfamiliar maze, and the farther she'd ventured, the more she'd veered off course. Now she was no longer entirely certain which direction was which.

Shade darkened the sky as she quickened her pace. The air was stale and murky. *This isn't the right way.* She stepped around a thorn bush, took out her cell phone, and waved it in the air in hopes of securing service. *Nothing.*

Whispers sounded behind her, and she spun around. There was no one there.

"Hello?"

A crow cawed, startling her. There were dozens, all perched across the bare branches above, staring at her. No—staring *past* her. That was when she noticed the cave entrance. The towering rock face nearly blotted out the sun, and the entrance cast a broad shadow over the earth.

Awed by its size, Brooke backpedaled. Something echoed from inside the cave. She listened carefully, and her brow furrowed. Were those more whispers?

Before she could investigate further, dry leaves crunched behind her. The crows took flight, as if something had frightened them away. Brooke turned her head to look for what had disturbed the birds.

"Is someone there?"

There was no answer.

The wind rose to a low moan. There it was again—the unmistakable feeling she was being watched. Brooke scanned the forest for anything out of place amid the falling leaves.

Footsteps approached. She wasn't alone. Either her friends were playing a prank or there was someone else with them in the forest. When she remembered the figure she'd spotted outside the cabin the night before, a chill crept down her spine. Brooke dropped to a crouch, hid behind the nearest tree, and waited. The hammering pulse in her ears threatened to drown out the footsteps, and she forced herself to keep calm.

After a moment, the footsteps faded. Perhaps the stranger—whoever he was—had gone. Brooke cautiously stuck her head out from behind the tree to make sure she was alone, and her gaze fell on a man lurking in the shadows around the cave. Falling leaves obscured his face. When Brooke saw the rifle he carried, she uttered an involuntary gasp before she could stop herself. She clamped a hand over her mouth, but it was too late. The stranger started toward her.

Brooke threw herself forward. She only knew one thing for certain—she needed to find help. The neighboring farm they'd passed on the way to the cabin was the safest bet. It lay just outside the forest. As long as she kept running, she'd find it eventually. Whoever her pursuer was, there was one thing he hadn't counted on: she was the captain of her school's track team.

When a gunshot reverberated through the air, Brooke nearly jumped out of her skin. The bullet missed her by only a small margin and scattered yet more crows to the wind. Brooke picked up her pace. Gathering speed with each step, she didn't look back.

No more gunshots followed. She kept going for what felt like at least an hour until she lost all track of time. Finally, just when her legs were about to give way, Brooke spotted the farm beyond the forest's edge. She stumbled past the trees, and the crows flocked overhead to follow her to the farmhouse that loomed above the crops.

Brooke hurtled through rows of corn. As she emerged from the cornfield, she cast a final glance back at the forest to see if the shadowy pursuer had followed her. There was nothing there.

The others are still out there. It struck her that, having failed to catch her, the stranger might go after her friends. *I have to get help.*

Surely there would be a landline at the farmhouse. She could call for help. Brooke froze when she saw the front lawn. When they first drove up to the farmhouse only one day ago, the yard had been virtually abandoned. Now, dozens of vehicles were parked outside the house. All the lights were on inside and emitted a strange glow under the darkening sky.

The familiar sensation of warning returned, but Brooke battled it down. The people inside that house were her only hope. She couldn't let anything happen to her friends—to Josh. She threw open the screen door and banged on the door.

"Help me." Her voice dissolved into sobs. Footsteps sounded inside the house, and suddenly she found herself face-to-face with the same old woman who greeted them the day before.

"You came back." For some reason, the woman didn't look particularly surprised. "He said that you would." Before Brooke could inquire further about the strange words, the woman ushered her through the doorway. "There, there, come inside. What's wrong, my child?"

"Please." Brooke's words tumbled out. "You have to help me. My friends are out there, and there's someone following us through the woods." She grabbed the old woman's arm to emphasize her point. "He had a rifle. You have to call the police."

"Of course." The woman attempted a smile presumably meant to put her at ease. "Why don't you have a seat at the kitchen table? I was just making some tea."

Brooke followed her into the kitchen. "There's no time."

The old woman gestured for Brooke to take a seat. "There's always time for tea." She spoke with a cheeriness that bordered on the unnatural. Why wasn't she more concerned?

Exhausted from her sprint across the field, Brooke practically collapsed into the chair. "Thank you."

"It's no bother." The woman poured tea at the counter behind Brooke's back. She set a steaming cup at the table and put a hand on Brooke's shoulder. "Now, don't you worry—I'll phone the police right away. You sit here and try to stay calm."

Brooke sighed. Her pulse had finally started to steady. She took a sip of the tea, which tasted surprisingly bitter. Still, her throat was parched, so she choked down another warm mouthful and listened to the woman's voice coming from the adjoining room.

What's taking her so long? What if the man comes back? She shuddered at the thought.

More voices were audible inside the house, and Brooke suddenly remembered the cars she'd seen parked outside. She frowned and glanced at the door to the next room. Someone had left it slightly ajar. Faint light glowed from inside, where candles burned atop some sort of altar. Brooke stole forward for a better look. Dozens of individuals kneeling in front of the altar were chanting something in a foreign tongue. Judging by the strange symbols on the altar, they weren't followers of any religion she was familiar with.

Something wasn't right. Brooke glanced back at the kitchen counter, and her gaze fell on a phone. If the old woman had wanted to make a call, she didn't even have to leave the room. Brooke picked up the phone and held it to her ear. To her growing horror, there was no dial tone.

The hair on the back of her neck stood on end. *I have to get out of here—now.*

Brooke started out of the kitchen, but her movements were sluggish and disoriented.

The old woman barred her path. "You weren't thinking of leaving, were you?" Her false smile faltered. "You're the guest of honor, after all. We have special plans for you."

"What did you do to me?" Brooke's speech became slurred. Her legs wobbled, and it took everything she had to remain standing. "The tea. You put something in it, didn't you?"

Then the world faded away, and everything went black.

Reagan, hurrying through the woods, tried desperately to keep up with the others. Things definitely were not going her way, and all because Little Miss Perfect had to go and get herself lost. It was almost worth it, the idea of Brooke stumbling around somewhere, alone. The thought made her smile.

Her sides ached from the trek through the forest. Despite her trim figure, Reagan wasn't particularly athletic, and the hike was taking its toll. She called out as the others threatened to pull even farther ahead. "Wait!"

The guys ground to a halt and turned back to check on her.

"Are you okay?" Josh started toward her, but Chad cut in front of him.

"Just give me a minute." Panting for air, she stopped and leaned against a tree for support. "I need to catch my breath."

"We have to keep going," Nick said. "The cabin can't be far."

Reagan glared at him. Josh's moody older brother had hardly said two words to her, but it was clear he didn't like her. Well, the feeling was mutual.

"Do you think you can tough it out?" Josh stared past her, deeper into the forest. "You heard that gunshot. We need to make sure Brooke is okay."

Reagan pursed her lips. Now Josh was taking Nick's side over hers? "Doesn't anyone want to talk about what we just saw back there?" She straightened her back. "That was a mass grave, Josh. *Human* graves."

Chad nodded. "That was seriously messed up."

She could always count on him to back her up. Her boyfriend might be a handsome idiot, but he certainly had his uses. Unlike the relationship she shared with Josh, an intense emotional and intellectual connection, Chad served more as a status symbol for her to show off. True, they also shared an undeniable physical attraction, but he was just one of many in her life who fit that description. In contrast, Josh, who offered a truly beautiful mind, never bored her.

"The handprint on the door." Nick turned to Josh. "Do you think they're connected?"

Reagan narrowed her gaze in Josh's direction. "What handprint?"

Josh bit his lip. "There was a handprint on the cabin door when we arrived. It looked like it was left in blood."

"Why are we only just now hearing about this?" She redirected her anger for failing to notice the mark herself to Josh.

Chad, as if to remind everyone he was capable of having his own thoughts, interrupted. "Don't forget the guy Brooke thought she saw in the woods last night."

That appeared to register with Josh. "Reagan, I need you to think carefully. Are you absolutely certain you didn't see anyone at the pond last night?"

Reagan suddenly found herself on the defensive. "Maybe."

It had felt so good watching Brooke squirm when Reagan had lied earlier, saying that seeing someone in the woods was just a joke. She hated how Brooke followed Josh around with puppy-dog eyes while flaunting her moral superiority over everyone else. Like she was any better. Reagan recognized jealousy when she saw it. Other girls had always been envious of her—of her looks, of her intelligence, but mostly because of the way men wanted her. Chad, Josh, and so many others—Reagan had them eating out of the palm of her hand, and she knew it. Unlike so many girls her age, *she* wasn't afraid to embrace the modern era. She wanted it all, and she wasn't afraid to take it.

Still, it grated on her that Brooke somehow believed the length of her friendship with Josh gave her a claim over him. Reagan didn't doubt this disappearing act was merely a ploy to attract attention and garner sympathy. Now she would actually have to pretend to feel sorry for her.

"Is that a yes or a no?" Nick's tone issued an implicit challenge.

"It means I wasn't sure." She turned to Josh. "I guess there could have been someone there. It was dark, and I could barely see anything. When I looked again, whoever it was had gone."

"Great." Chad began pacing. "My freaking vacation, and there's a stranger chasing us through the woods."

"Everyone, calm down." Josh crossed his arms. "We don't even know for certain that shot had anything to do with us. It could be a hunter. Maybe someone thought Brooke was trespassing and wanted to scare her off. For all we know, Brooke might be at the cabin right now, waiting for us."

"And what if she's not? If those stories about the disappearances are true, we can't just stick around and wait for her." Reagan touched Josh's arm lightly, the way she always did when she wanted his attention. "Josh, tell them we need to leave."

The gesture was clearly not lost on Chad, who nevertheless agreed with her. "Let's get in the car and leave right now. Once we reach the highway, we can call the police. Let them handle this."

For a moment, Josh didn't appear quite so enamored of her. "We're not leaving Brooke behind. Period."

Reagan released her grip, and his arm fell away.

Nick started down the trail. "Come on."

Reagan followed as the others took off sprinting for the cabin. Just when she thought she couldn't go any farther, the cabin materialized through the trees.

Brooke was nowhere in sight. The campsite was abandoned. The fire pit had been reduced to ash. Even the crows were gone from the trees.

Nick hurried into the cabin before emerging moments later. "She's not in here."

Chad called to them from beside the vehicles. "Hey, guys. Check this out."

Someone had slashed their tires.

This isn't happening. The hair on Reagan's arms stood on end.

"We need to be careful." Nick studied the slashed tires. "Something odd is going on here."

Josh scratched the back of his head. "We still have to find Brooke. We can worry about everything else later."

"And how are we going to do that?" Reagan demanded. "On foot? Brooke could be anywhere! We'll never find her."

"Let me think. Where else would she go, if she was looking for a safe place?

Reagan and Chad exchanged glances, and the answer came to her at once.

"The farm."

Chapter SEVEN

Brooke woke with a start.

Where am I? Her thoughts were still clouded.

Then she opened her eyes, and it all came rushing back. She remembered seeking shelter inside the farmhouse after fleeing her mysterious pursuer through the woods. The bitter taste of the drugged tea lingered on her lips.

Bumps broke out on her arms in response to the cold. Brooke tried to move and realized she was tied to a chair. Her hands were bound behind her back. A flickering fluorescent light intermittently illuminated the room's shadowy contours. *What is this place?* Brooke slowly took in her surroundings. A narrow stairway across from her led to a door above. The floor was bare cement. Brooke guessed she was locked in the cellar. She was alone, at least for the moment.

The old woman's words came back to her. "We have special plans for you."

What did she mean by that? The light flickered again, and Brooke noticed blood, black under the fluorescent radiance, splattered across the cement walls. Rows of bloodstained tools, including rusted saw blades, hammers, and pliers, hung from the walls. The sight of chains and ropes piled in the corner gave her pause, but it wasn't until Brooke spotted a tooth on the floor that she began screaming at the top of her lungs.

"Help me!"

No one came, no matter how many times she called for help. The walls were probably reinforced to prevent sound from escaping. Whoever had locked her in the cellar didn't want her getting out.

Who are these people? Brooke shuddered as she recalled the strange pagan symbols in the candlelit room. Suddenly, the lack of keepsakes and pictures inside the farmhouse made sense. *This isn't a home at all.* It was a compound, one that housed a cult of some kind. They were hidden in the mountains of Appalachia, where no one would ever think to look for them—and where no one would ever find her. Judging by the tooth on the floor, Brooke wasn't their first victim.

I have to get out of here. As her mind cleared from the adrenaline, Brooke scanned the room for anything she could use to escape, and her gaze fell on a round saw blade on the wall at her back. She wriggled in her seat to inch the chair backward. If she could catch her ropes on the blades, maybe she could cut herself free.

After several excruciating minutes, the chair hit the wall. Just as she felt the blades grate against the ropes, groaning floorboards, accompanied by heavy footsteps, came from above. *Someone's coming.* Brooke worked to free herself with new urgency.

The door to the cellar swung open. The old woman, now adorned in a flowing black robe, observed her from the top of the stairs.

"Don't bother screaming." The woman's wrinkled mouth twisted into a taut grin. "There's no one around to hear you but us."

"Who are you? What do you want from me?" Brooke's heart pounded as the woman approached until she stood mere inches away.

"Don't despair, child." The old woman reached out to her. Brooke shrank from her touch, but the woman ran a hand through her hair, prompting a shiver. "You have been chosen."

Brooke stared past her, where more figures in robes had appeared on the stairs. Hoods obscured their faces. "It's time. He's ready for her."

The old woman let her hand fall away and pulled a hood over her face.

"Chosen for what? Who's ready for me?" Brooke fought against her restraints, but they held her still and forced a blindfold over her head.

Someone removed the ropes around her chest and ankles, though her hands remained bound behind her back. Someone prodded her forward, and she stumbled up the stairs.

She heard the screen door open, and the procession filed outside the house. Thunder rumbled faintly in the sky, and Brooke felt the cool air against her skin. She peeked at the ground from under her blindfold in hopes of catching a glimpse of where they were leading her. She wanted to make a run for it, but she saw swishing black robes everywhere she looked.

Brooke's gaze moved from the dirt trail at her feet to green rows that shot up from the ground. *They're taking me into the cornfield.*

They led her deep into the cornfield, to a place where fallen stalks were arranged in a circle around an open space. In the center of the circle was a stone table surrounded by candles and what she hoped were animal bones. A pole stuck out of the ground behind the table. There was something mounted on the pole, but the blindfold prevented her from getting a good look at it. A goat bleated nearby from where its lead rope was fixed to the table. An empty bowl sat at the end of the table beside a stone dagger.

It wasn't a table at all, she realized. It was an altar.

Brooke broke free and bolted toward the rows with the intent of fleeing into the cornfield, but a pair of strong hands grabbed her from behind.

"Tie her down," someone said.

Brooke, kicking and clawing, was forced onto the altar against her will.

Someone removed the blindfold from her face. The wind fell, and a disquieting hush settled over the farm. Suddenly, the cultists parted on two sides, and a man in bright red robes stepped forward. Although his head was uncovered, an elk skull masked his face. Its horns cast a shadow over the ground. The edges of the man's robes were blurred, as if he were a wraith caught between this life and the next.

"The time has come." He lifted his hands and spread them in the air, and the others bowed low to the ground and began to chant.

Brooke collapsed against the stone altar and finally saw the thing mounted on the pole.

The face of a scarecrow stared back at her. Its stitched mouth was frozen in a malevolent grin.

Oh my God.

She screamed, and her cries faded into the cornfield.

By the time they reached the farm, the world had changed. Storm clouds approaching from all sides smothered the dying light. A blood moon, so large it almost appeared within reach, hung heavy above. Then there were the crows, raging everywhere through the sky.

Nick, hidden in the trees, stared across the field in disbelief.

Reagan shifted uncomfortably beside him. "What the *freak* is going on?"

Nick couldn't have put it better himself. "Nothing good."

The birds flocking overhead began to circle the cornfield. The hair on the back of his neck stood on end at the sight of even more crows perched along the fence. They littered the farmhouse and watched, almost as if they were expecting something.

"We have to find Brooke," Josh said.

Nick, unable to pry his eyes from the apocalyptic scene, remained silent. *I have a bad feeling about this.*

Chad appeared uneasy with the suggestion. "Do you really think she's there?"

Nick offered his brother his support. "It's our best chance to find her. If Brooke isn't there, we can always use their phone to call for help."

"Let's go." Josh stepped out of the forest and beckoned the others.

Nick walked side-by-side with him, while Chad and Reagan followed behind reluctantly. It was at least a half-mile hike from the woods to the farmhouse, which took on a sinister appearance under the bleak sky. They walked along the cornfield on a dirt path while the breeze swept fallen leaves as it howled past them.

Nick's brow furrowed. "Did you hear that?"

"Hear what?" Josh's attention remained fixed on the farmhouse, less than fifty yards away.

"It sounded like someone screaming."

"I didn't hear anything." Reagan looked as if she would rather be anywhere but where she was at that exact moment.

Josh lowered himself into a crouch. "Get down." He took refuge within the cornfield, and the others quickly did the same.

Nick whispered, "What is it? What did you see?" He spotted two figures in black robes vanishing down a path into the cornfield.

"What are we still doing here?" Reagan demanded. "Normal people don't dress like that." She shot Chad a withering expression when he motioned for her to keep quiet. "We need to get out of here, now, before they see us."

Josh didn't budge. "We can't leave until we get Brooke back."

Chad shook his head. "Dude, did you see those robes? I don't think we want to mess with them."

"We'll have to be smart about it then." Nick leaned closer to Josh. "I have your back. What's our move?"

Josh took a moment to think. "Look." He pointed to the vehicles parked in the yard. "Chad, do you think you can steal one of those cars?"

"Yeah. If I can't find any keys left inside, I can hotwire one. My stepdad taught me how."

"Good. Reagan, you keep watch outside. Nick and I will sneak into the house to search for Brooke. If we find her, we're getting out of here."

The screen door opened again, and another hooded figure emerged from the farmhouse and disappeared among the cornstalks.

"Come on." Josh started to move, but Reagan grabbed his hand.

"Josh, it's too dangerous." She pleaded with her eyes. "We should leave while we still can."

Before Josh could answer, a scream reverberated from deeper within the rows.

"Brooke." Josh tore through the cornstalks with Nick following after.

Brooke found herself unable to look away from the scarecrow's sinister gaze. It looked down at her through a single button eye. Its lifeless arms were spread out like branches. In all her life, she had never seen anything more terrifying. Thick black stitches ran down its face and all over its body, which appeared to have been shredded and painstakingly sewn back together. Half of its burlap head was marred and blackened from burns.

A horrifying thought occurred to her. *What if Josh's stories were true?*

Brooke thrashed around desperately, and her attention returned to the man in the elk skull mask. "Who are you? What do you want from me?"

The man's voice made her blood run cold. "My name is Bartholomew. I am only a servant of a greater power." He pointed at her with a long, slender finger. "A power that will soon be awakened once more."

Bartholomew approached the stone table and took the ceremonial dagger into his hands. Brooke strained against the rope in an effort to pull away from him, but instead of reaching for her, he seized the goat by the neck and slit its throat. The dying animal collapsed into the dirt with a whimper. Blood spurted into the bowl, and the cultists' chants grew louder.

"Hear my cry, Keeper of the Crows." Bartholomew poured the blood over her, and Brooke shut her mouth and eyes as the warm blood splashed over her face.

"You're insane."

Bartholomew hardly seemed to acknowledge her. "Our moment has come, my apostles. Within these caves lies a gateway to Sheol. Jezebel Woods destroyed the fragment of our master's spirit that was trapped inside the cave, but she did not close the gate."

"Let me go." Brooke, straining against her bonds, came to an abrupt halt. Given her limited view, she was certain she had imagined it, but it almost looked as if one of the scarecrow's fingers had moved.

Bartholomew set the bowl aside and reached for a large, ancient-looking book bound in a black leather cover. "All the scarecrows were destroyed but one. Once we have restored it to life, it will complete the ritual and summon Baal through the gateway." He read from the book in a harsh tongue Brooke didn't recognize, and thunder clashed above.

The cultists prostrated themselves before the altar and the scarecrow that loomed above it. They spoke in unison. "Rise."

Brooke heard movement, and something rustled in the cornfield nearby. She glanced over and saw Josh and Nick watching her through the cornstalks.

"Help me," she mouthed as the worshipers chanted.

Josh whispered something to Nick, and Nick retreated and disappeared from view.

The chanting stopped. Bartholomew handed the book to a disciple and approached the altar. He towered above Brooke and raised the stone dagger high.

"With this sacrifice, we will reawaken our master and plunge the land into darkness!"

Chad didn't care for Josh's plan. Then again, he didn't care much for Josh himself. He liked that the guy was calling the shots even less.

I didn't even want to come on this stupid trip. He was only there because he wanted to keep an eye on Reagan. He knew how she got around Josh. Chad wasn't afraid to admit that he was jealous—Reagan was *his* girlfriend, after all.

Even though she could be a real pain sometimes, she made him feel different than any girl he had ever been with. That was why it was so hard to feel her pulling away. If it wasn't for the fact that Josh was screwing around with her, Chad might almost feel sorry for the guy. Once she was through with Josh, she would toss him aside. That was what she did.

Chad glanced back at the farmhouse, where Reagan remained on the lookout. She gestured to him that the coast was clear, and Chad, careful to keep low, crept across the yard.

More screams echoed through the cornfield, and Chad shuddered involuntarily. When he reached the parked vehicles, he eased open the door to one and looked inside.

No keys. He swore.

Voices sounded nearby. Three more figures in robes were headed his way. He glanced over at Reagan, who was also exposed. Just when he thought the figures were certain to spot him, they passed him by.

Chad let out a sigh of relief. He looked through three more vehicles before he found a truck with the keys inside, and his lips turned up in a smile.

Finally, some good luck for a change.

Brooke's breath caught in her chest. Before the man who had called himself Bartholomew could thrust the dagger into her heart, Nick leaped out at him, while Josh used his pocketknife to cut the ropes around Brooke's hands. Nick and Bartholomew struggled for possession of the dagger, and the knife clattered to the earth. Nick took a step back and looked down at the altar. Glaring at Bartholomew, he swept the candles off the stone table and kicked over the bowl of blood before smashing the bones. A low wind rose over the cornfield, and all the flames went out at once.

"You're too late." Bartholomew straightened his back as the other cultists rose behind him. "Your God has forsaken you. You will fail these people, just as you've failed everyone you care about."

Nick defiantly positioned himself between his brother and the cultists.

"And you, who have blood on your hands." Bartholomew's gaze turned to Josh. "Your mother died because you didn't act. Your father died because you did. What makes you think you can save *her*?"

Nick clenched his teeth. "Don't listen to him, Josh. He's trying to get into our heads."

"Fool. You understand nothing. Before the night ends, each of you will die, and there is nothing you can do to stop it. Your deaths will resurrect this world's greatest evil." Bartholomew lowered his voice and hissed, *"Rise."*

When Bartholomew finished speaking, a shadow fell over the earth. In the sky, the blood moon crawled across the face of the sun. The light faded, devoured by the total solar eclipse, and darkness fell over the earth.

Nick readied himself for a fight. "Josh, take Brooke and get out of here—now."

The last rope fell away. Still sitting on the altar, Josh's hands on her shoulders, Brooke's face froze, and an expression of pure horror overtook her.

Above the altar, the scarecrow slowly raised its head. For a moment, no one—not Nick, Josh, Brooke, or even the cultists—moved. Then the scarecrow unclenched its fist and began to wrench itself free of the post.

Josh held out his pocketknife to ward the cultists away and took Brooke's hand. "Run!"

The cultists moved too slowly to intercept them. As they darted past the rows, the last thing she saw was Bartholomew raising his hands, out-stretched to the dark, into the air.

Then she heard the rustling of wings.

What the heck?

It was as if all the color had drained from the sky. Chad squinted as he fumbled with the keys and attempted to find the ignition in the dim light. Nightfall wasn't for another few hours. Something was seriously messed up with this farm.

Chad slid the keys into the ignition and the truck roared to life. He flipped the headlights on, put the vehicle in reverse, and pulled around to pick Reagan up. Cultists, visible in the rearview mirror, came running from the cornfield.

Reagan sprinted toward the truck, tore the door open, and climbed inside. "Go!"

Chad shifted gears and slammed his foot on the gas. "What about the others?"

Reagan cast a fleeting glance at the cornfield as the truck turned onto the gravel road. "Just keep going."

Chad hesitated. Suddenly, a shadow fell over the ground. He looked up in bewilderment at the crows. All across the farm, they rose from their perches to form a massive flock the likes of which he had never seen.

Distracted, Chad veered off course. Before he could correct their trajectory, the birds descended and swarmed the truck. Cracks spread through the windshield, and Chad struggled to maintain control of the vehicle. It was nearly impossible to see where he was going amid the black cloud of crows.

Reagan grabbed his arm in a panic. "You're going to crash!"

Chad shook free of her grip. "I can't control it!"

She looked at him one last time before throwing open the door to the truck and jumping out. Chad reached for her, but she was gone, lost to the blackness.

The crows peeled away one by one, giving him just enough time to see the side of the barn before the truck struck it head-on.

Brooke and Josh fled across the cornfield to escape the crows. Nick, enveloped by the storm, had already vanished. The birds shrieked as they plunged from the sky one by one, and Brooke clutched Josh's hand and held on for dear life.

He squeezed back firmly. "Hold on, Brooke. We have to keep going."

She cast a glance over her shoulder. The birds were almost upon them. "Josh."

The swarm engulfed them before he could answer, and suddenly she could no longer see him. Brooke struggled forward, but there were too many crows. Josh's grip weakened, and he was torn away from her, leaving her grasping empty air.

Chapter EIGHT

Josh had faced death before.

After Nick left home, their father got worse. He was always quick to anger, but something had changed. The beatings were more brutal than ever. In the old days, Josh's dad used to apologize after an episode. There would be a brief interval where he tried in vain to turn over a new leaf. That part—the part of his father Josh once loved—was gone. In its place was a haunting, dead look in his father's eyes.

Josh was in his second year of high school when it happened. His father had lost his job by then due to frequent absences from work, so Josh took to cutting class to check on his mother. He made her promise to lock herself in her room whenever his dad returned from the bar, but that day, for whatever reason, his dad came home earlier than usual.

Josh's mother was still alive when he found her. Josh begged and pleaded to no avail. He tried to fight off his father, but the man was driven by an insane, drunken rage. When all else failed, Josh trained a gun on his father and told him to let her go.

Josh would never forget the terrible silence that followed. Time seemed to slow inside the house. He looked at his father, and his father looked back at him, all while his mother's whimpers grew fainter. The gun shook wildly in Josh's hands. He didn't think he could do it—he didn't *want* to do it. Then his father raised his fist and stepped forward, and Josh pulled the trigger. His father died instantly. Josh's mother passed on the way to the hospital. Orphaned, Josh went to live with his aunt, and nothing was ever the same again.

He'd lived through one nightmare only to find himself in another. When he saw the scarecrow come to life, he couldn't help remembering the last time he faced down a monster, and he knew he could do it again. Although Josh didn't fully understand what was happening, he was determined to figure it out so he could put a stop to it and save his friends—whatever the cost. Right now, that meant finding Brooke.

She had been right there with him only moments ago, before the mass of crows descended on them. Then she was gone, lost somewhere inside the vast cornfield. Nick, behind them mere moments ago, had also disappeared amid the storm of wings. Josh glanced up at the sky, where the crows continued to gather above the cornfield, and ran between the rows searching for Brooke. He turned this way and that, but the dense cornfield was a maze. Even from the woods, the cornfield seemed to stretch on without end.

She could be anywhere. For that matter, so could he. Josh couldn't see anything beyond the sea of cornstalks—not the forest, the farmhouse, or the gravel road. He wasn't entirely sure where he was.

"Brooke!" His voice echoed across the rows and faded into the dark. Josh slowed his pace and listened. He heard only the wind rustling through the stalks. Josh gritted his teeth. Brooke wasn't the only one around who might hear him. The dim imprint of footprints in the dirt stared back at him from the ground. Josh bent low and touched the fresh prints with his hand. They were Brooke's size.

Following the tracks, he rounded the corner and froze. The scarecrow loomed a short distance ahead with its back to him.

It's following Brooke's trail. Josh's fist curled up in a ball. With the scarecrow's back turned, he had the advantage. He was the taller of the two. How strong could a heap of straw be? He readied himself to unleash his pent-up rage.

Josh paused. The scarecrow was supernatural, and he had no idea of the extent of its abilities. He was alone, with no weapons. If he attacked and failed, there wouldn't be a second chance. Josh had seen too many horror movies where impulsive decisions got people killed. He needed to play this smart. There were more lives at stake than just his own.

I have to get to Brooke before the scarecrow finds her. If they could make their way out of the cornfield, they could search out the others and regroup. Then he would try to come up with a plan. Hoping to retreat before the scarecrow saw him, he crouched low and took a few steps back.

"You there!" a voice rang out from the end of the row, where a cultist had spotted him.

At the sound of the man's voice, the scarecrow turned around, and its awful gaze fell on Josh, who stared back at its sinister button eye.

Run. He took off in the opposite direction. His momentum carried him forward into a collision with the cultist, who reacted too slowly. The pair lost their footing and crashed through the cornstalks into the next row, where Josh dropped his pocketknife.

A low hiss echoed from deeper within the cornfield, and the hair on the back of his neck stood on end. Josh pushed himself up, but before he could get away, the cultist grabbed his ankle and pulled him back to the ground. The man pounced on him and grasped for Josh's pocketknife, which lay inches away. Josh reached out desperately and took hold of a rock buried in the dirt. He brought it up hard against the cultist's head and scrambled back. The robed assailant started toward him, but the scarecrow's hand shot out of the stalks and pulled him into the depths.

Josh snatched up the pocketknife and took off running with the cultist's screams reverberating through the night.

Chad woke to the sound of the diesel engine, which continued to run, oblivious to the sorry state of the truck. He let out a low moan and opened his eyes to discover himself slumped over the steering wheel. A wooden beam was lodged in the windshield, mere inches from his head. If the truck hadn't come to a stop when it did, the broken beam's pointed end would have pierced his skull.

Jolted awake by the surge of adrenaline, Chad jerked his head back. Shards of glass from the windshield were scattered across the front seat. Dead crows stared back at him lifelessly from the other side of the glass. There were black feathers everywhere.

Chad ignored the ringing in his ears and removed his seatbelt. His entire body ached from the violent collision, but at least he was still in one piece.

"Reagan?" There was no response. He gazed over at the passenger side, which sat empty. *She left me.* She hadn't hesitated before bailing to save herself. Reagan was gone, and she hadn't even come back to see if he was all right.

Chad rolled over in his seat and opened the door. Disoriented, he promptly tumbled onto the ground. The ringing in his ears slowly subsided, and he shakily climbed to his feet. The night stole into the barn through a massive hole in the wall behind him. The truck and the barn had done considerable damage to each other.

This is all Josh's fault. Josh was the one who insisted on a spooky Halloween camping trip. He thought he was so clever with his little map, but really he'd just managed to drop them all into the middle of a horror story. Who knew what had happened to him, or any of the others?

Chad heard shouting outside the barn. Recovered enough from the crash to remain mobile, he inched forward while hooded figures hurried around the property.

They're searching for us. Chad weighed his options. From what he had already seen, it was pointless to go up against the cultists. There were too many. No, he needed to get away from the whole crazy area as soon as possible. *The gravel road is the best choice.* It led back to the main road. Maybe he'd worry about finding help for the others later, after he was safe.

Chad kept low and watched the figures outside the barn. Whatever all the commotion was about, it was clear something major had just happened. He glanced at the sky, where the crows flocked above them. What was up with that? There was no *way* that was normal bird behavior.

His gaze fell on the remaining cars parked in the yard. With any luck, he'd find another one with keys inside, and then . . .

One of the cultists pointed in his direction. "Over there!"

Having noticed the damage caused by the crash, they started toward the barn. Chad swore and sprinted past them into the field. Certain a star athlete could outrun anyone in flowing robes, he veered onto the gravel road and ran like his life depended on it.

Another figure stepped out of the cornfield to block the path. Kicking up gravel, Chad ground to a halt and pivoted in the opposite direction. His pursuers converged on his location and surrounded him on nearly all sides. As they closed in around him, Chad raced toward the farmhouse. A cultist at his back grabbed at his shirt, but Chad connected with a blind punch, tore free, and stumbled inside the screen door.

He ran through the parlor while trying to decide which way to go.

"He went this way!" someone yelled behind him.

Chad started to panic. He didn't know the layout of the house, and with the cultists hot on his trail, he didn't have much time to look. His gaze fell on a door at the end of the hall. He threw it open and raced to the bottom of a flight of stairs, only to find himself with nowhere to go. He had stumbled into the cellar, and now he was trapped.

Chad spun around, but the cultists had already found him. Three hooded figures descended the stairs. Chad flung himself at them but was easily overpowered.

"Hold him steady." A figure forced him against the wall. As Chad struggled to wrest himself free, the overhead fluorescent light flickered, and the robed figure lifted a hatchet from the wall. The man started toward him and raised the hatchet high. Then, suddenly, everything went dark.

Reagan fled deeper into the woods. She hadn't looked back when she first stumbled past the border of the trees, and she didn't plan on starting now. The others were gone, lost somewhere in the swarm of crows that had covered the farm. She was alone. Then again, she had always been alone.

Reagan was only a girl when her mother was hospitalized. Schizophrenia—that was what the doctors called it. To a child, it simply meant her mother was gone. The woman barely even recognized her. She was somewhere else, *someplace* else. They locked her mother away in a padded cell when Reagan was only eight years old.

She slipped on a rock and lost her footing before catching herself on the ground. Reagan unleashed a string of profanities and steadied herself against a tree. The forest was darker than she remembered. It was nearly impossible to see anything. The eclipse seemed to have swallowed the very stars from the sky.

There was no solar eclipse scheduled for today. Reagan, who regularly killed time scrolling through local weather and interesting headlines on her smartphone, couldn't recall any mention of an expected celestial event. As she continued at a more careful pace, she thought again of the hooded figures and the screams coming out of the cornfield. Then there was the strange behavior of the crows. *What's going on here?* She'd stumbled into a nightmare, only she couldn't wake up from it.

"You're losing it, Reagan." She bit her lip. Now wasn't the time for self-doubt. She needed to be strong.

After her mother was hospitalized, Reagan bounced around from foster home to foster home. She never stayed in one place for any length of time. No one wanted her. In time, she learned to start looking out for herself first. Even when she was finally adopted, Reagan continued to find it difficult to trust anyone.

As she grew older, and boys began paying more attention to her, she learned that she could use her natural good looks and intelligence to her advantage. None of the boys really meant anything to her. They were a means to an end; namely, her own enjoyment. If she didn't care about anyone, it wouldn't hurt to lose them. Forced to choose between the others and herself, she would choose herself every time with no remorse. Whatever had happened to Chad, Brooke, Nick, or even Josh, was no longer her concern. At the moment, the only thing that mattered was survival.

The crows hadn't followed her into the woods. That was one good sign at least. Something rustled in the bushes behind her. Reagan, aware of the possibility that one of the robed figures had followed her into the woods, froze for a moment and listened. The sound stopped.

I knew there was something wrong with that farm, she thought, remembering the lack of animals in the barn and the absence of mementos inside the house. She supposed the robed figures were devil worshipers of some kind. *This wouldn't be happening if the others had just listened to me. But no, they decided to be heroes. Well, look where that got them.*

Think rationally. What was the safest course of action? There was no telling how many cultists there were in total. She had seen at least five already, in addition to the old woman they'd met the day before. As long as Reagan remained out in the open, she would be exposed, no matter how far she delved into the woods. The answer was clear. *I need to find a place to hide.*

She pushed deeper. Hadn't Josh said something about caves in the woods? Perhaps she could seek refuge in one, if she could find it. The forest changed the farther she went. The air was thicker. The towering trees bent and swayed in the wind like sleeping giants. Their empty branches seemed like claws stretching toward her. Gleaming animal eyes watched her in the dark. Reagan stumbled into a spider web, which clung to her hair no matter how hard she tried to sweep it away. When she jerked her face away from the web, she noticed a light farther ahead.

What's that? She peered into the dark. She was too far away to make out the source of the distant illumination. Reagan crept closer while remaining careful to keep out of sight among the trees. There, in a clearing, a small hut was hidden in the woods. Firelight glowed from a single dust-covered window. The chimney spurted black smoke into the air.

It was deathly quiet. Only her footsteps made noise. Reagan surveyed the property. In addition to the hut, there was a chicken coop and a modest garden, as well as a stack of lumber beside a group of tree stumps. A creek flowed behind the hut. She looked around. Given the absence of a vehicle, she surmised no one was home. The presence of the fire and smoke suggested whoever lived there had left relatively recently, and there was no telling when they might return.

Although there were no telephone lines in sight, it was possible there was a radio or something else she could use to call for help inside. Perhaps whoever lived there would help her. Reagan cast a long shadow over the yard as she left the safety of the trees behind.

From the outside, the hut looked impossibly old. It was in better shape than the cabin, but not by much. Moss and vines growing along the sides ate away at the few flecks of white paint that remained on the wooden exterior. Reagan glanced over her shoulder to make sure she was alone and walked up the steps. For a moment, she felt as if someone was watching her.

She thought about knocking on the door but instead grabbed the doorknob and slowly twisted it open. The door fell ajar with a creak to reveal a single room bathed in the fireplace's glow. Grateful for the warmth provided by the flames, Reagan gently shut the door behind her and advanced inside.

She examined the hut in the firelight. A rifle sat propped against the wall beside the door. There were no phones or radios anywhere that she could see. In fact, there were hardly any signs of technology—not even so much as a flashlight. It was as if the hut existed outside of time. Everything inside was antiquated and out of date. There was no fridge that she could see. There wasn't even a bed—only a small cot in the corner of the room.

How can someone live like this? She stared at a jar where a pair of dentures was suspended in murky water. Disgusted, she wrinkled her nose.

Then she noticed the newspaper articles. The faded, yellow clippings, barely legible in the dim light, were spread out across the walls. Reagan approached the wall and squinted in the firelight. Several of the newspapers were from the early twentieth century.

There was a town here once. She quickly scanned the articles. From what she could tell, the neighboring coal mines had been closed after someone discovered the entrance to a cave on the property. Her gaze fell on the picture of a young woman accompanying a more recent article.

Local Woman Still Missing. Police are continuing the investigation into the disappearance of local resident Kara Healy, who along with her husband Ethan, has not been seen in four weeks. They were last believed to be camping in rural Appalachia.

The article was dated five years ago. There were others too, going back as far as fifteen years. Reagan remembered the mass graves they'd discovered earlier that day, and she thought again of the gunshot they'd heard.

I need to get out of here. Right now.

At that moment, footsteps sounded outside the house. Reagan froze. She looked around desperately for somewhere to hide, but there was nowhere to go. Before she could make a run for the gun, the door swung open.

Chapter NINE

With crows at his back, Nick staggered out of the cornfield. He hit his knees and gasped for air as the birds flocked through the cornstalks before taking to the sky.

"Josh?" He waited for Josh and Brooke to emerge behind him, but the cornstalks remained still. There was no hint of his brother concealed in the dark spaces between the rows.

They were right there. Until the swarm separated them, Josh and Brooke were almost within his reach. *I have to find them.* No matter what had happened between them, Josh was still his brother. Josh needed his help, and Nick wasn't about to let him down. Not this time.

Nick stared ahead at the farm. For all he knew, Josh and Brooke could be anywhere. Maybe they'd escaped the cornfield already. He stumbled to his feet. His clothes were torn and dirty. Scratches marred his skin where the birds clawed and pecked at him, but for the most part, he was unharmed. He narrowed his gaze at the sky, where the swarming crows' dissonant shrieks carried across the farm. Whatever force was controlling them, it wasn't natural. Something dark was at work—something evil.

Nick knew it the moment he and Josh had interrupted the ritual. This was not an ordinary cult of lunatics who cut themselves off from society like he'd seen in documentaries. This was a more sinister group. Something else nagged at Nick's memory. The cult's leader seemed to know him and Josh without ever having met them. How could he have known what happened to their parents? It was impossible. Not only had the cult leader raised the scarecrow to life, he'd also called down the crows. And his dark power unnerved Nick.

Whatever the cult is planning, it must need us dead to complete the ritual. He wasn't going to let that happen—not to Josh or anyone else.

He debated whether or not to search for Josh and Brooke on the farm or re-enter the cornfield to find them. Neither option was particularly appealing. The cultists patrolled the farm, but the scarecrow was somewhere in the cornfield. *A living scarecrow.* He wouldn't have believed it if he hadn't seen it with his own two eyes.

Shouts rang out across the field before Nick could decide which way to go. He followed the commotion to its source, where Chad was sprinting down the gravel road toward the farmhouse with cultists in pursuit.

What are you doing? Not that way! Chad had already disappeared inside the farmhouse. Once the cultists caught up to him, he'd be cornered like a rat in a cage. Praying he could reach Chad in time, Nick flung himself forward and ran as hard as he could.

When he entered the farmhouse, he caught a glimpse of a black robe disappearing around the corner, where an open doorway loomed at the end of the hall. A shout rang out from below, and Nick peered down stairs awash with flickering light. Two cultists held Chad pinned against the wall while a third approached with a hatchet. As the robed figure raised the hatchet into the air, Nick switched off the cellar's overhead light and plunged the room into darkness. Using his cell phone's flashlight for illumination, he rushed down the stairs and grabbed Chad by the arm.

Nick felt Chad stiffen at his touch. "It's me," he said before Chad could pull away. "This way." They ran up the stairs with the cultists close behind. Just as Nick neared the doorway, a hand grabbed him by the ankle. He managed to kick himself free. The moment he crossed the threshold, Chad slammed the door and bolted it shut.

They're not getting out anytime soon. Nick stared at all the locks. The cellar had been built to keep prisoners locked inside. It wasn't hard to guess why.

Stripped of his false bravado, Chad sank to the floor and started shaking while the cultists banged against the door from the other side.

"They were going to kill me." He was clearly struggling to comprehend the situation he found himself in.

Nick bit his lip and glanced down the hallway. Aside from the cries of those down below, there wasn't a sound in the house. They were alone—for now. He squatted beside Chad and grabbed his shoulders. "Snap out of it. We have to stick together if we're going to make it out of this."

Chad, as if noticing him for the first time, stirred. "You came back for me."

"Have you seen Josh and Brooke? I couldn't find them."

"No. I'm sorry."

"What about Reagan? You two were together."

"She left me." Chad's voice betrayed obvious bitterness. "I found a truck that would get us out of here, but I lost control of the wheel when the crows swarmed us. Reagan jumped out before it crashed."

"What about the rest of us?" Nick released his hold on Chad. "You were just going to leave us?"

Chad lowered his head and mumbled something unintelligible. Nick climbed to his feet. There wasn't time to explain to Chad what had transpired in the cornfield. Besides, he wasn't sure Chad would believe him.

"We can't stay here. There'll be more of them soon. We have to search for the others and find someplace safe." Nick gestured for Chad to follow him and retraced his steps through the parlor. The house groaned from the sweeping winds outside. As they made their way to the front door, he spotted cultists approaching from across the yard.

Nick's jaw tensed, and he dropped out of sight to avoid being seen. There were too many.

He lowered his voice to a whisper. "We might be able to make it to the cornfield before they see us."

When he turned around, Chad was gone.

Brooke couldn't see Josh anywhere. The crows had taken him from her, and now she was alone again. Or perhaps she wasn't so alone after all. The cult—not to mention the scarecrow—was still searching for her. She wished it was all a dream, that she could pinch herself and put an end to it, but there was no waking up from the nightmare in which she found herself.

Something rustled within the tall rows at her back. Brooke spun around but was greeted only by darkness. Cornstalks surrounded her on every side. The flowing green leaves waving at her beckoned her deeper into the cornfield.

"Josh?" *It was probably nothing—just an animal or the wind.* Brooke winced when recalling the stone dagger inches from her heart and the elk skull staring down at her. She did her best to block out the horrifying images and kept going.

The trip was supposed to be an opportunity to get away from it all. It was her last chance to reconnect with Josh before Reagan's claws went in too deep. Brooke had promised herself during the drive from Louisville that she was finally going to tell him how she really felt. She was sure he knew, but it had always gone unspoken between them. Now it was probably too late. Maybe it didn't matter. How many times before had she made up her mind to do the very same thing? In the end, this trip probably wouldn't have turned out any differently.

Brooke wished she were fearless like Josh and Reagan. She would even settle for some of Chad's bluster. All her life, Brooke had lived with the fear that she couldn't measure up. It probably started when her father left. Brooke tried her best to help her single mother take care of the family, but it wasn't easy. Her mother was rarely home, a consequence of working three jobs.

That left Brooke to take care of her sister, Harper, born with Angelman Syndrome, a rare genetic condition that affected her nervous system. Although Harper suffered from a severe intellectual disability and frequent seizures as a result of her condition, Brooke almost never saw her sister without a smile. She was seemingly always happy. Given the opportunity, Brooke wouldn't change a thing about Harper, but that didn't make taking care of her any less of a challenge.

On top of everything else, she still had to juggle school. While she wasn't brilliant like Josh or Reagan, Brooke studied hard and made good grades. She ran track to unwind, or at least she used to, until her mother started a new job that meant Brooke needed to stay home with Harper after school. It was a sacrifice she was happy to make because Brooke believed in doing the right thing and putting family first. She was a good person, but sometimes she couldn't shake the feeling that wasn't quite good enough.

Brooke groaned. No amount of selflessness was going to help her in finding her way out of the cornfield. Yet another row confronted her everywhere she turned. A sudden chill permeated the air, and she shivered involuntarily. Brooke wrapped her arms around herself for warmth and felt gooseflesh crawling across her skin. The cold air rendered her breath visible in the dim light.

Wings beat at her back, and a tall shadow crept across the ground. Startled, Brooke hurried the other way only to come face-to-face with the scarecrow at the end of the row. She ground to a sudden stop in the dirt. The scarecrow's shuffling gait reminded her of a reanimated corpse. Paralyzed by fear, Brooke couldn't move as the scarecrow drew closer until at last only the night was between them.

Josh's voice rang out from among the rows. "Brooke, get back!"

Josh came sprinting from the next row. The scarecrow let out a hiss and twisted to meet him. Brooke found her footing and scrambled back, but she couldn't bring herself to leave Josh, who hurled himself at the scarecrow. It lifted him in the air like he weighed nothing and swung him off his feet. He hit the ground hard.

"Josh!" Brooke rushed to his side. "Get up." She attempted to help him to his feet as the scarecrow approached. Before Josh could regain his footing, the scarecrow grabbed Brooke's wrist and jerked her forward with a bloodstained hand.

Josh lunged at it from the ground. "Get away from her."

The scarecrow released her at once and seized him by the throat. Brooke struck it from behind, but the scarecrow sent her crashing to the ground with the back of its hand. Josh gasped for air, and their eyes met as he struggled in vain to free himself from the scarecrow's unbreakable grip.

Suddenly, two more figures came crashing through the stalks. Brooke recognized Nick, locked in a struggle with a hooded cultist with a torch. The pair landed on the ground in a heap beside Josh and the scarecrow.

Nick struck the cultist across the face, snatched the fallen torch from the ground, and waved the flame at the scarecrow, which shrieked and relinquished its grip on Josh's neck to shy away from the fire.

"You don't like fire, do you?" Nick put himself between them and the scarecrow and held the torch out like a ward against evil.

The scarecrow, wary of the flames, loomed above him but did not advance. Its malevolent burlap face glowed in torchlight that highlighted the charred portion where it had been burned before.

Brooke rushed to Josh's side and helped him up. "Are you okay?"

"I'll live." His voice was weak.

Nick cast a glance at the fallen cultist while keeping an eye on the scarecrow. "Get to the woods. The cultists are everywhere."

Brooke followed his gaze and saw specks of firelight visible through the stalks. "What about you?"

The scarecrow drew nearer as voices approached. It was growing bolder.

"Don't worry about me. I'll be right behind you."

"If we get separated, meet us at the cabin." Josh took Brooke's hand, and they fled through the cornfield together, until the rows swallowed the light behind them.

A towering figure loomed in the doorway, masked by the shadows. He stood there for what felt like ages and stared at her from the dark. When he stepped into the firelight, Reagan's heart skipped a beat. The man across from her was even taller than Josh. Unlike Josh, who had a lean frame, this man was built like a monster.

Long, thinning black hair, greasy and matted, fell over his face in patches. He wore a pair of faded coveralls and mud-stained boots. Cruelty was etched into his scarred face, and his fingernails were untrimmed and grimy.

There was only one reason she could think of why the stranger would have kept the newspaper clippings about the missing campers. Reagan was almost certain the identities of the skeletons buried in the graves they discovered earlier matched the names in the articles. Her attention fell on the rifle, which lay tantalizingly out of reach. The stranger's mouth twisted into a cruel smile of rotted teeth poking out from anemic gums.

Reagan took a step away from him, and her back brushed against the wall. There was nowhere to go. The night called to her from the open door, but the stranger's massive frame blocked her only route of escape from the hut. He closed the door and plunged his hand into the jar with the dentures, as if daring her to make a run for the gun.

Reagan remained rooted to the spot, her mind racing furiously. *I have to be careful.* The stranger held all the cards, and they both knew it. Antagonizing him was the last thing she needed to do.

"You must be lost." His voice had a heavy country twang. His face was even more gruesome with the dentures in place. The crooked, yellowed teeth were at least one size too big for his mouth. "What's a pretty thing like you doing out here in the woods, all by your lonesome? It's not safe out here, so I hear."

Her skin crawled as his eyes wandered over her, and she fought to stay strong. Suddenly, Reagan regretted not telling the others the truth earlier. If she had backed up Brooke's story, maybe she wouldn't be in such a mess.

"I'm not alone." The lie came easily to her. Most lies did. "We're looking for our friend. She's lost."

His eyes seemed to see right through her. "At least your friend had the good sense to run away. Of course, running won't do her much good. She was heading in the wrong direction."

Reagan looked around for anything she could use against him. There was a poker in the fireplace, if she could get close enough to use it. *I have to keep him talking.* "The devil worshipers. Are you one?"

He laughed, a harsh sound that made her stomach drop. "Hardly. I was here long before their lot showed up. They don't even know I'm here." He took a step toward her.

"Wait." She held up a hand in protest. "My name is Reagan. What's yours?"

His eyes shone with sinister delight in the firelight. "I reckon there's no harm in talking. It gets lonely out here sometimes. The thing in the cave doesn't talk to me like he used to. The name is Wyatt."

He's insane. Reagan couldn't reason with him, but perhaps she could play into his delusion. "The thing in the cave?"

"The Natives believed this land was cursed." Wyatt watched her carefully as he spoke. "They thought evil spirits fed off the blood shed in these hills. My father was a coal miner. He stayed on the land after the mine was shut down, even after the others left. I was a boy when I found the entrance to the cave. It showed me the truth—showed me how to play the game." He stared past her into the flames. "My father didn't like the game very much. I killed him first."

She gestured to the newspaper clippings. "You murdered all these people?"

"They all lost the game." He paused. "Aren't you going to ask me what I want?"

"I think we both know what you want."

"I saw you in the water last night. So pretty. So full of life." Wyatt unsheathed a blade strapped to his waist, and the serrated knife shimmered in the dim light. "I wonder if you're just as pretty underneath your skin."

Reagan kept her back to the wall. If she could just reach the door, she could make a run for it. "I want to play the game with you, but you have to give me a chance. It can't be much fun for you otherwise."

He sneered. "I wonder how long you'll make it. The longest one lasted for two weeks."

"I can help you. My friends are still out there. I can lead you to them. Maybe we can even kill them together."

Wyatt stopped. "No one's ever said that before."

Reagan snatched the poker from the fireplace and swung it at him. He caught it easily, and the poker clattered to the floor. Wyatt lifted her from the ground with one hand wrapped around her throat and tossed her onto the dusty, timeworn rug. Reagan, feigning unconsciousness, waited motionlessly on the ground for him to approach. At the last moment, she thrust out her leg. Wyatt tripped, lost his balance, and fell face-first into the fire.

Reagan scrambled wildly to her feet and flung open the hut's door as Wyatt's screams filled the air behind her. Just as she reached the edge of the trees, she glanced back and saw him at the top of the steps, pointing the rifle in her direction.

The blast reverberated through the forest.

Chapter TEN

They ran hand in hand through the dark. Josh glanced over his shoulder and searched the rows for Nick, but his brother was gone. He didn't even want to think about Nick's odds against both the scarecrow and the cult. Josh wanted to go back, but he couldn't—not with Brooke counting on him.

He noticed bloodstains all over her. "Are you hurt?"

"The blood isn't mine. That maniac poured goat blood all over me." Brooke paused. "Nick's still back there."

She was trying to hide the fear in her voice. Given all she'd been through, it was a wonder she was on her feet at all.

"We have to keep moving. The end of the cornfield can't be far."

"Those lunatics are everywhere. What are we going to do?"

"We go back to the cabin and regroup. If any of the others made it out, maybe they'll meet us there. I won't let anything happen to you, Brooke. I promise."

He meant it. Brooke was the only one who had been there for him after his parents died. Josh didn't have many friends at that point. He'd always been bookish and introverted. With his parents dead and Nick gone—his brother didn't even come to the funeral—Josh had been almost completely alone. The death of one parent was hard enough, but having to deal with killing his father? It was almost too much to endure. If it hadn't been for Brooke, Josh probably wouldn't have made it.

Nothing was ever the same for him after his parents' deaths. Before that night, Josh had always been an optimist at heart. Despite all the abuse he'd endured, he always held out hope things would get better. That part of him died when he pulled the trigger. He gave up on the idea of a loving God. Josh decided that, in the grand scheme of things, life was a mostly meaningless search for fleeting happiness. So many people chose to cling to delusions rather than avoid facing that simple truth, but Josh embraced it. It was a depressing thought, to be sure, but then again, he *was* being treated for clinical depression.

Brooke's grip tightened around his hand. "Over there—there are more ahead." True to her words, torchlight glowed through the stalks.

Josh led her another way, but there, too, he saw flames in the night. They were cornered. It wouldn't be long before someone in the cult spotted them.

Brooke squeezed his hand and pointed across the rows. "I can see trees!"

He followed her gaze. The woods, visible just outside the cornfield, promised safety. They brushed past the stalks and started toward the trees.

Whispers spread through the cornfield like laughter, and the crows rose behind them. Josh saw a flash of movement a short distance away, where a shadowy figure darted through the rows.

We're not alone.

The scarecrow's face leaped out at him from the darkness. They crashed through the rows in a mad dash to safety, and Josh lost his balance and spilled onto the cold earth outside the cornfield.

The scarecrow, now carrying a pitchfork, stepped past the corn. The blood moon reemerged behind its back, and the scarecrow's shadow fell over Josh.

It reached for him, but Brooke grabbed his arm and pulled him to his feet, and together they stumbled toward the woods. Then the scarecrow lifted its hands toward the moon, and the crows shot toward them as one.

Chad kept running. He didn't plan on stopping anytime soon. Not until he reached the road, anyway.

He felt a pang of guilt for leaving Nick behind, especially after Nick put himself in danger to rescue him from the cult. Chad knew it was wrong, but he had done it anyway. It was hardly the first time. That was supposed to make it easier, wasn't it? Chad pictured the cultists, their torches blazing against the night sky, converging on the farmhouse with Nick trapped inside.

Sometimes he wished he could be more like Reagan. She never cared who she hurt. Nothing ever bothered her. Sure, she paid lip service to any number of political activist causes, but Reagan really only cared about herself. Not that he was any better. While the cult was focused on Nick, he had used the opportunity to slip out the side door.

I left him there to die.

When more cries rang out from the cornfield, Chad forced himself to ignore them. There was nothing he could do for the others anyway.

As it turned out, going out the side door was a stroke of luck. A narrow path between the cornfield and the forest's edge extended the length of the farm. Unlike when he ran down the gravel road earlier that night, there was no one around to see him. The tall rows kept him hidden from sight. The cult was occupied with the farmhouse or the cornfield. No matter how many cultists there were, they couldn't be *everywhere*.

A harsh shriek carried across the farm from the cornfield.

What was that? It definitely didn't sound like anything human. Suddenly uneasy, Chad peered into the rows. His gaze fell on a shape at the cornfield's edge, and he nearly tripped over himself in surprise. When he looked back, the figure was gone.

It was probably nothing. His mind was playing tricks on him. It wasn't surprising. Although Nick hadn't explained what went down inside the cornfield, it was clear from the look in his eyes that something seriously disturbing was going on. Yet another reason Chad needed to get out while the getting was good.

Grateful for all those extra laps his coach made him do when he was caught cheating on his geometry final, Chad gulped down another lungful of air and charged down the path against the harsh wind. The black rail fence loomed ahead, less than half a football field away.

Caws sounded above, where a group of crows had diverted from the main flock and now approached from over the cornfield. The birds— were they actually *following* him? No—they couldn't be. That was insane, wasn't it?

They're just birds. He remained unable to shake the image of the swarm that caused his wreck. *Don't lose your cool, not when you're so close.*

The rail fence was almost within reach. A fog settling over the road covered everything beyond the fence. Chad slowed his pace, climbed over the wooden fence, and dropped onto the other side, finally free of the farm. Soon, it would all be a distant memory.

The temperature plunged without warning, and Chad found himself shivering. He wandered into the thickening mist, which clung to him and impeded his movement. His shoes touched pavement, and Chad realized he was standing on the road. He squinted in the dim moonlight to discern his surroundings. It was nearly impossible to see anything in the mist.

Chad reached into his pocket and took out his cell phone. *Still no service.* He switched on the flashlight. It wasn't much compared to a real flashlight, but it was better than nothing. A few yards away, the light reflected off a yellow road sign warning of a sharp turn ahead.

Footsteps sounded on the road behind him.

"Guys?" There was no response. Maybe the cultists had followed him—but how? He was careful not to be seen.

There it was again. Chad wheeled around and pointed his light at the noise's source. The beam fell on the crows, which sat perched in a line along the fence, their black eyes regarding him through the mist.

Then he heard something scraping along the road.

"Who's there?" Chad swung the light around, and the beam fell on a figure dragging a pitchfork behind it. To Chad's horror, he realized the thing wasn't a man at all.

The scarecrow remained motionless. Its face fixed on him. Unlike the typical generic scarecrows he remembered from countless fall festivals, this one looked like something straight out of a nightmare. Insects crawled from holes between its stitches. Its hands looked like claws.

"You're not real." Chad took a step back, and the scarecrow receded into the mist. The crows swarmed around him, and Chad swatted them away while stumbling through the fog. The birds scattered and left him alone once more.

Chad pointed the light into the fog and sought out the scarecrow, but it was gone. He took another step back and brushed against something firm behind him. Trembling, Chad slowly turned around and found himself staring into the scarecrow's horrifying face. Before he could react, the scarecrow hit him in the mouth with the pitchfork's handle. Blood streaming from his lips, Chad toppled to the pavement.

His gaze fell on the rail fence. The forest loomed on the other side, just out of reach. Chad crawled toward the fence while the scarecrow approached at his back. The moment his hand grabbed the wooden plank, the scarecrow drove the pitchfork into his ankle. Chad screamed and released his hold on the fence. The scarecrow tore the pitchfork loose, grabbed him by the ankle, and pulled him back into the fog. Chad clawed at the earth, but the scarecrow's grip was too powerful.

The scarecrow knelt low until its face was inches from him. At the last moment, Chad remembered the electronic cigarette in his pocket. He grabbed it and stabbed it into the scarecrow's face, burning a hole where its missing eye once rested. The scarecrow let go of him with a shriek, and Chad rolled underneath the fence. Leaving a trail of blood behind, he climbed to his feet and limped away into the forest. When he glanced back, the scarecrow had disappeared once more into the fog.

The torches glowed brighter. They were gaining on him. Nick ran this way and that, but there were more cultists wherever he turned, and the stalks themselves seemed to close in around him. Nick hesitated and cast his torch aside. Although it was his only defense should the scarecrow return, the firelight drew too much attention.

He tried to remember what had happened to the scarecrow after the cult converged on him, but everything had happened so fast that it remained a blur.

I have to reach Josh and Brooke. It was a nice thought, but he felt no closer to navigating his way out of the cornfield than before. At least he had the moonlight to guide his path.

Nick rounded a corner and practically ran straight into one of the cultists. He narrowly managed to elude the hooded figure's grasp, but the cultist waved his torch in the air and yelled to alert his companions to Nick's presence. Nick threw himself into the next row and looked over his shoulder in time to see the cornfield awash in torchlight.

Sweat poured down his brow. The crows danced above like living shadows against the backdrop of the blood moon. Stalks rustled behind him as footsteps approached nearby. Hoping they couldn't hear his ragged breaths, Nick dropped to a crouching position and hid. His carotid pulse pounded so hard it hurt his neck.

The footsteps drew closer, and several hooded figures passed by, silently waving their torches in the air. Nick stayed perfectly still as each went by in succession. He was certain they would notice instantly if he moved an inch.

One of the cultists stood mere inches away—so close Nick could have reached out and touched the hooded figure's robe. The cultist's torchlight ate into the shadows that kept Nick concealed. Ready to spring forward if they spotted him, he mouthed the words of a prayer, and miraculously, the hooded figure left to join the others.

"This way!" one of the figures shouted. "They're running toward the woods!"

Josh and Brooke. Nick kept low and followed the sound of the voices. Before long, he glimpsed the forest through the cornstalks. The cultists stood with their backs to him between the cornfield and the trees.

One cultist gestured to the others with his torch. "Spread out. They could be anywhere."

Nick waited until the hooded figures dispersed. When the torchlight faded into the woods, he stepped free of the cornfield and started toward the trees. He was fairly certain he could find his way back to the cabin in the moonlight.

"You'll never reach them in time." Red robes flowing in the wind, the man in the skull mask held a long scythe in his hands. Reverberating from somewhere underneath the elk skull, the man's bone-chilling voice shattered the stillness of the night. "Your friends are as good as dead."

"You're lying." Nick waited for the cult leader to attack, but the man remained where he stood.

"You should have let us have the girl. By interrupting the ritual, you've condemned them all. The scarecrow won't stop until you are dead."

"It's already killed at least one of your followers too. You can't control it, can you?"

Harsh laughter roared above the wind. "The others are but pawns—meaningless. With each life the scarecrow takes, it grows stronger."

Nick backed into the shadows. "It doesn't matter. My brother and the others are already on their way to safety."

"They will never leave these woods alive, and neither will you." The figure raised the black book, and shadows seemed to pour from it as he uttered words in a harsh tongue that drove into Nick's mind like a splinter. Fog pouring over the rail fence obscured the world beyond the farm.

"What have you done?" Nick, reeling, struggled to keep his grip on reality.

"The darkness will keep you trapped in these hills until dawn. I doubt you'll last that long."

"You won't win. I'll find a way to stop you."

The wind died low, and a hush fell over the woods.

"I am much older than you, and my master is older still."

Nick charged forward in an attempt to catch him off guard, but the figure burst into crows, leaving Nick to wonder if he had ever really been there at all.

Chapter ELEVEN

10:11 P.M.

When she left the others and sought refuge in the forest, Reagan thought she was leaving the madness behind. Instead, she found herself drawn even deeper into it. Because she had been so quick to abandon their dead weight, she was now vulnerable on her own, stalked by Wyatt.

Reagan slowed to a crawl and listened for her pursuer. *Nothing.* Aside from muffled thunder and the creek's gentle murmur, the forest was utterly still. Even with the full moon hanging overhead, the dense trees blotted out most of the light. As her eyes adjusted to the pale glow, Reagan pushed through the brush as quietly as possible in case prying ears were nearby.

Unlike her mother, who had completely lost touch with reality, Wyatt was a different kind of crazy—a murderous psychopath who had her locked in his deadly game. Now that she had provoked him, he wouldn't rest until she was dead.

I have to get out of here. But that was easier said than done. Even if she wanted to, she couldn't return to the farm—not because of the cult, but because she didn't know the way. The group barely had time to explore the woods during the light of day. How was she supposed to find her way in the dark? Meanwhile, Wyatt was certain to know the layout of the land by heart.

Maybe I can find my way back to the cabin. If any of the others survived their ordeal at the farm, the cabin was the most likely place they would return to. Wyatt would remain no less a threat to a group, but at least there was safety in numbers.

The hilly terrain proved even more difficult to navigate than she anticipated. She frequently tripped over roots and stones in her path. She was tired, sweaty, and covered in dirt. This was not how she planned to spend her weekend. *This is the worst fall break ever.*

She approached a small clearing where fewer trees limited her places to hide. The creek's flowing waters sparkled in the moonlight. *Follow the water to its source.* She remembered reading that in a book somewhere. Exposed under the blood moon, Reagan splashed across the creek and started uphill.

A twig snapped where she had just been, and Reagan stiffened. Something moved toward her through the brush. She hid in the tall grasses, covered herself in the pile of fallen leaves under one of the massive oaks, and waited.

For several moments, she heard nothing. *What if I was imagining things?* She was in enough trouble without her mind playing tricks on her. She was about to move from her hiding place when a long shadow fell over the ground. Wyatt was barely visible among the trees. The towering figure slowly advanced through the clearing in search of her. His face was covered by darkness, but she was sure the flames had left their mark.

"Reagan." His voice echoed through the clearing, and for a second, she thought he had spotted her. Her skin crawled at his proximity. He dragged a chain behind him in the dirt and carried the rifle in his other hand. It took all her restraint not to scream. "I know you're close. I can taste your fear."

Reagan did her best to remain motionless while her entire body yelled at her to run. Despite the insects crawling over her, she forced herself to stay calm.

"Maybe I should start with killing your friends. You didn't tell me their names, but I'm sure I can make them tell me themselves. I'll even let you watch."

He took another step forward, then one more, until he was standing almost on top of her. His enormous black boot rested mere inches away from her face. Reagan pleaded silently for him to move on, but Wyatt remained in place to survey the area.

"You can't stay hidden forever." Without warning, the lines of his face contorted in rage to give him an almost demonic expression. "Show yourself!"

Reagan trembled involuntarily at the sudden display of rage. Just when she thought she could remain still no longer, Wyatt walked away and headed downhill. She let out a deep breath and waited for her thundering heartbeat to quiet.

That was too close. The savagery in Wyatt's voice was unmistakable. She didn't want to think about what he would do to her if he caught her. After the sound of his footsteps faded, she lay there for several minutes longer until she was certain he was gone. Finally, she sat up, brushed herself off, and climbed to her feet.

That was when she heard him. Wyatt stepped out from behind the trees, where he had hidden in the shadows. He had doubled back so stealthily that she hadn't heard him until it was too late. Unable to speak, she stared at him in the moonlight. Wyatt's lips pulled back in a twisted grin as he approached while swinging the chain like a lasso.

Reagan bolted, but she was too late. The chain hit her hard in the back, and she went rolling downhill. Before she could pick herself up, a hand grabbed her shirt and pulled her effortlessly from the ground.

"Let me go." She fought in vain to escape his grip.

Wyatt's lips brushed against her ear as he spoke. His foul breath felt hot against her neck. "And let you tell your friends about me? That would ruin the game, and I have plans for them too." He held her from behind as she struggled.

"I wouldn't tell anyone. I swear."

"Don't worry—they'll join you with the others in the ground soon enough. We can't have police poking their noses where they don't belong." He clamped a hand over her mouth. "Don't bother screaming. There's no one around to hear you."

"Reagan?" The voice came from a figure at the top of the adjoining hill, barely visible through the brush.

Chad. With Wyatt distracted, Reagan sank her teeth into his hand and bit down hard, drawing blood. Wyatt's grip slipped, and she broke free. "Chad!" She scrambled uphill toward him. "Over here!"

She looked back and saw Wyatt, chain in hand, moving through the darkness. She stumbled and nearly slid down the steep hill. Grasping a tree trunk to steady herself at the last minute, she clawed at the muddy earth to keep from sliding down. There was nothing left to anchor her along the peak. Although she was near the top, her pursuer was steadily gaining on her. Just before she lost her balance, a hand shot out of the night and took hold of her.

"Reagan." Chad pulled her over the side. "Thank God."

Chad grimaced, and she saw blood near the bottom of his jeans. "What happened to you?"

"You would know if you hadn't left me." He made no effort to hide his anger. "How could you? I thought we were in this together."

Reagan pushed him away. "We don't have time for this. We're not alone."

"I know—the scarecrow could be anywhere."

"Scarecrow?" Her brow furrowed. "There's someone else out here. He's been stalking us through the forest."

Chad looked perplexed, but before he could open his mouth to respond, something moved in the brush, and three hooded figures with torches emerged. One started toward them with a knife.

"They're mine." Wyatt, looming behind Reagan and Chad, trained his rifle on the cultist with the knife. The cultist froze, and he pulled the trigger. The blast rippled through the air and knocked the robed figure with the knife off his feet.

The remaining cultists exchanged glances, and one held his torch aloft and took a step closer. "Leave this place or die, hillbilly. Their blood is ours to shed."

Wyatt spun the heavy chain in the air. "I've always wanted to kill one of you."

Reagan squeezed Chad's shoulder. "We have to go." She sprinted blindly through the woods as Wyatt descended on the cultists. Chad, slowed by his injury, limped behind her.

The trees parted ahead to allow moonlight to spill inside the forest.

"Look." Chad pointed to the ground, and Reagan followed his gaze to the same set of railroad tracks they discovered earlier that day. "I know where we are."

Brooke hadn't meant to fall in love with Josh. She wasn't even sure when it happened. They had been best friends since grade school, which seemed like a lifetime ago as she ran beside him under the blood moon.

Josh came to a stop a short distance ahead and studied the forest quietly. "Is something wrong? Are we lost?" Brooke bit her lip and glanced back, waiting for the scarecrow to jump out at them at any moment. Despite her fears, the woods were quiet—almost unnervingly so.

"We should be heading in the right direction." Josh pointed out a path to her. "I think this is the trail we took to find you earlier. It should lead us back to the cabin."

Josh had always been a natural adventurer. He loved exploring the wild and frequently talked Brooke into tagging along on his expeditions when they were kids. They were so inseparable that Brooke's mother once called them twins.

Then puberty made a mess of everything. They had just started high school when Brooke started to realize she thought of Josh as more than a friend. She grappled with these new, confusing emotions, unable to decide whether or not to share her feelings with him. She didn't want to risk losing their friendship, after all.

The forest grew denser the farther they traveled from the farm. Brooke guessed they were at least a mile away from the cornfield, if not more. Although each step away from the farm brought her more relief, she couldn't help feeling more than a little uneasy at the prospect of wandering through the forest with a living scarecrow lurking somewhere in the dark.

Something rustled on the tree limbs above, and when she looked up, she saw dozens of crows watching them. The sight made the hair on the back of her neck stand on end.

"Any sign of Nick?" Josh asked.

"Not yet."

Josh's face was an expressionless mask, but she knew what he was thinking. After all the things Josh said about him, Nick had put himself in harm's way for both of them. Although it seemed almost impossible that he could have escaped the cornfield with the cultists on his trail, she didn't plan on saying so to Josh, who had already lost both his parents.

Brooke had almost worked up the courage to tell Josh how she felt about him when his parents died. With Nick out of the picture, Brooke was the only person Josh had left. He was vulnerable enough without her complicating things further.

Killing his father had devastated Josh. He told her the other students in his school treated him as if he were a delicate glass that might break if not handled with care. Others still were afraid of him or whispered terrible things behind his back.

Brooke could do little more but watch as a moody pessimist slowly replaced the cheerful, positive Josh she once knew. And yet, there were still hints of him in there. Josh was the only friend who had never treated Harper differently than anyone else. Although his parents' relationship had taught him to keep his guard up, the kindness with which he treated Harper revealed an inner goodness that no amount of trauma could erase.

Brooke had every opportunity to tell Josh how she felt, but she'd waited too long, and he met Reagan.

Josh brushed a branch out of his way. "I think we're getting close."

The sound of crunching leaves was faintly audible in the distance. Brooke, trailing at Josh's side, searched for the source of the sound. For a moment, she thought she saw a brief glow through the brush, but then it was gone.

Josh's voice startled her. "We're here."

The campsite, visible through the trees, lay quiet under the moonlight. The cabin loomed in the shadows. The dead of night amplified its sinister appearance. Everything was preserved exactly as they left it. The campfire, long dead, was a composite of soot and ash. Their vehicles sat just off the road. The tires had all been slashed.

"All our gear is inside." Josh headed for the cabin. "We'll barricade the door and wait for the others before we decide what to do."

A horrible thought dawned on her. "Josh, what if we're the only ones left?"

He didn't answer.

Brooke heard the sound of someone approaching from the woods. *We're not alone.*

Josh held his finger up to his lips to indicate he'd heard it too. "Quick. Inside."

Brooke kept her eyes on the woods. Josh eased open the cabin door so they could slip inside, but before he closed it again, Brooke discerned the dim outline of a robed figure standing at the border of the campsite. She inched away from the door and kept the figure in view through the window. After regarding the abandoned campfire for several moments, the cultist made his way over to the vehicles to inspect the slashed tires. His gaze fell on the cabin, and Brooke—almost certain that he'd seen her—dropped out of sight.

For a moment, all was quiet. Then she heard the unmistakable noise of his footsteps crossing the yard. Josh, who had hidden behind the couch, motioned for her to join him. Brooke crept across the floor, but the door opened slightly before she could reach him, and she instead hurried to the kitchen, which was closer.

Moonlight spilled into the dark room, and Brooke pressed herself against the kitchen counter. The wooden floorboards creaked under the figure's boots. His hood slowly turned in her direction, and before Brooke could get away, he lunged forward and grabbed her by the hair. A knife was clutched in his hand.

"Brooke!" Josh slammed into the cultist from behind, and the collision carried them into one of the kitchen shelves. Falling jars broke as they struggled, and the hooded figure struck Josh across the mouth and forced him back over the counter.

"Josh!" Brooke pulled at the figure's robes and caused the hood to fall away. Josh clawed at the man's face as the cultist slowly forced the knife into his shoulder. Brooke rushed at the man at the same time Josh kicked him. The cultist stumbled into the doorway and grabbed at Brooke, but Josh pushed her out of the way at the last moment.

The cultist raised the knife, but before he could stab Josh a second time, he toppled over and collapsed to the floor.

Nick, holding the rusty axe from the lumber pile outside the cabin, stood behind him in the doorway.

Chapter Twelve

10:51 P.M.

Despite their circumstances, Nick couldn't help smiling at finding his younger brother unharmed. He offered his hand, which Josh regarded for a moment before taking it, and Nick helped him to his feet.

"You're alive." Josh didn't bother hiding his disbelief.

"Luckily for you. You didn't think I was going to let a few crows keep me from rescuing your sorry rear end, did you?"

Josh's face darkened. "I never thought I'd say this, but it's good to see you, Nick."

"You too, little brother." Nick paused after noticing the bloodstains on Josh's shirt. "You're hurt."

"It's only a flesh wound." Josh winced as he moved his shoulder. "I'll be okay." He retrieved the fallen knife from the unconscious cultist and slid it under his belt.

Brooke hurried to greet Nick. "How did you make it out of the cornfield?"

"I ran and didn't stop running." Nick glanced around the cabin. "Any sign of Reagan or Chad?"

Josh shook his head. "Not yet."

The wind picked up outside the cabin and made the trees bend and sway in its wake. Outside the doorway, dozens of crows lined the trees surrounding the cabin. All the birds were looking in their direction. Nick shut and locked the door as Brooke switched on the lantern.

Josh and Nick dragged the cultist to a corner of the room and tied him up with rope from Josh's supplies.

"What now?" Nick tested the rope to make sure it was tight enough. "I've been so busy running, I hadn't really thought that part out yet. We're in big trouble here, and I hope you have a plan."

The moment Josh opened his mouth to speak, someone banged on the cabin door from the other side. Everyone tensed at once. Josh quietly approached the door with the cultist's knife in hand. Nick picked up the axe and nodded to Josh, who threw open the door. Reagan and Chad rushed into the cabin before he could strike, and Nick lowered the axe in relief.

"I'm so glad you're okay." Josh wrapped Reagan in a tight hug as Brooke watched with a decidedly unhappy expression.

When Reagan's gaze fell on the robed figure propped up against the wall, she immediately let go of Josh and took a step back. "What the freak is that?"

"We have him tied up. He can't hurt us."

"Like that makes her feel any better." Chad slammed the front door shut. "If one of them found this place, the others can too. We can't stay here."

Nick felt a sudden surge of anger at Chad's attitude. "So, you just want to run again?" He grabbed Chad's collar and pinned him against the wall. "I came back for you, and you left me to die."

"Is that so?" Reagan put her hands on her hips. "Then why did you give me such a hard time, Chad?"

Chad averted his gaze. "I was scared."

"Enough." Josh raised his voice to get everyone's attention. "This isn't going to work unless we stick together. We have to have each other's backs."

Nick released Chad but glared at him for good measure.

"Do you know how many horror films I've seen?" Josh paced the floor. "More than you can count, and in every movie, it's always the same story. The campers get separated from the group and the killer murders them one by one. We have to be smarter than that if we're going to make it out of this."

"What do you suggest, genius?" Chad tried to put an arm around Reagan only to find himself rebuffed.

"We start by figuring out what the heck is actually going on." Josh turned his attention to Brooke. "Tell us what happened after you went missing earlier."

"There was a man in the woods with a rifle. He started chasing me, and I ran to the farm to get away."

Nick stroked his chin. *That explains the gunshot we heard.* "Was he one of the cultists?"

Brooke appeared unsure. "I don't think so. I didn't get a good look at him."

Reagan interrupted. "His name is Wyatt. He's the one who slashed our tires. He was watching us in the woods last night. The graves we found—he killed those people. That's what he does. It's all a game to him."

Brooke raised an eyebrow. "Graves?"

"We found a mass burial site after you went missing." Josh's focus remained on Reagan. "If this Wyatt isn't one of the cultists, who is he?"

"He said he's been here a lot longer than they have. I found his hut. There were dozens of newspaper clippings inside. There used to be a town around here back when the mine was still running. Wyatt's father was one of the coal miners. This guy is seriously disturbed. He believes there was something in one of the caves that used to talk to him."

Chad gritted his teeth. "You're telling me there's someone *else* who wants us dead?"

"That explains the disappearances in the area over the years," Josh said. "Brooke, what happened when you reached the farm?"

"The old woman we met the day before drugged me, and the others tied me up. They're some kind of cult. Their leader—Bartholomew—said he planned to sacrifice me to the Keeper of the Crows."

"The man in the elk skull mask?"

Brooke nodded.

"Hold on." Reagan looked skeptical. "You've got to be joking. The Keeper of the what?"

Brooke shrugged. "Bartholomew said its name is Baal."

"Baal." The name struck a chord with Nick. "That name belonged to a false god in the Old Testament." He stiffened when recalling all the supernatural events that occurred since they interrupted the ritual.

"Bartholomew said something else," Brooke added. "He claimed the caves contained a gateway to some place called Sheol."

That stopped Josh in his tracks. "Sheol is the Hebrew word for the underworld. Why would he say that?"

"I don't know. He said a woman named Jezebel Woods tried to get rid of Baal's sprit, but they were going to use the ritual to bring him back."

Josh froze.

Nick turned to face his brother. "What is it?"

"Jezebel Woods was the name of the sheriff who went missing in Gray Hollow. I remember it from Reddit. Brooke, can you remember anything else about Bartholomew?"

"He had a strange book with him. He read from it in another language before the eclipse started."

Nick snapped his fingers. "It must be some kind of spell book. I crossed paths with Bartholomew before I caught up to you. He used the book to create a mist over the road. He said we'd be trapped here until the ritual was complete."

"A *spell book*?" Reagan looked at Nick as if he were crazy. "Come on—are any of you actually buying this? I hate to break it to you, but there's no such thing as magic, whatever they taught you in Bible school."

Josh looked at her sheepishly. "Reagan, there's something you need to know. When we went into the cornfield to rescue Brooke, the cult leader was about to offer her to a scarecrow."

"Like the ones from your story?" Her eyes were full of disbelief.

"It's not just a story," Brooke said. "I watched it come to life."

Chad nodded eagerly. "It's true. That thing tried to kill me earlier."

Reagan backed away from the group. "This isn't happening. It's not real."

"It *is* real. Denying it won't make it go away." Nick kept his voice firm. "And it's not going to stop until we're all dead—not unless we figure out a plan. It wouldn't hurt to say a few prayers either."

Josh looked incredulous. "Praying? You can't be serious."

"Why not? If supernatural evil exists, then why can't God?"

"Then where is He? If God is real, then let him show Himself." Josh gestured to empty air. "I don't see anything, Nick. You should spend less time praying to a fantasy and more time trying to help."

"Nick is helping," Brooke protested. "He's already saved both our lives, and unless you've forgotten, I'm a Christian too."

"Yeah, but—"

"But what? I'm not a genius like you or Reagan, so it's okay for me to have delusions?"

Josh held up his hands in protest. "Look, all I'm saying is we need to use logic."

Chad laughed. "Bro, we just saw an actual scarecrow come to life. I think logic just went out the window."

Reagan again interrupted. "Enough bickering. I, for one, am not planning on dying here. I'm also not waiting around for some imaginary entity to rescue us. So, what are *we* going to do to get ourselves out of this mess?"

"This is bigger than us," Nick replied. "Whatever this cult is planning to unleash, I don't think it's going to settle for the five of us. We might be the only ones who can stop them."

Josh clearly wasn't convinced. "We have no idea what we're up against. I think the best course of action is to keep going in the opposite direction from the farm. We still have our phones. I say we walk until we either get reception or find help."

In other words, he wants to run rather than stand and fight. They might not give us that option. Josh's plan made sense if they merely wanted to survive, but Nick couldn't help remembering what Brooke had said about the cult's attempt to summon forth a demon from hell. *Someone* had to do something about that.

"How are we supposed to know where to go?" Chad asked.

Josh rooted around in his bag until he found a compass. "We'll use this." He took out the map of the area he'd shown them the previous night and spread it over the kitchen table. "We'll go east. This trail should lead us the closest to civilization."

"I agree," Reagan said. "We shouldn't stay here long. Let's gather what supplies we need and leave."

Chad limped across the room and collapsed onto the couch while Josh handed out flashlights and continued rifling through his bag. "Wow. We really won the Halloween lottery."

"What happened to your leg?" Nick asked.

"Pitchfork." Chad wore a resigned expression. "I'm a star receiver, and now I can't even run. What use am I now?"

"I'm an EMT. Let me take a look at that." Nick bent down beside Chad and fought the urge to grimace at the gruesome injury. "How's it holding up?"

"It hurts every time I try to walk, but I've played through worse pain before."

Nick finished inspecting the wound. "You got lucky. It could have done a lot more damage. I think I can bandage this up." He glanced over at his brother. "Josh, toss me the first aid kit." He dug through the kit until he found bandages and set about wrapping the wound.

Chad held his breath for most of the process. To his credit, he didn't let out as much as a whimper. "Thanks. I'm sorry I left you. It was a crappy thing to do."

"Yeah, it was. Then again, there was a time when I would have done the same thing in your shoes."

Interested, Chad leaned forward. "What changed?"

"I did." Nick stood and helped Chad up from the couch. "There. I can't say it's as good as new, but that's the best you're likely to get for now. If we make it out of this, you'll need to see a doctor to make sure it doesn't become infected."

Josh tucked a flare gun into his pocket. "Is everyone ready to go?"

Laugher emanated from the cultist they had tied up. "It's too late for you. You're all doomed. Nothing can save you now."

"What do you want?" Josh demanded. "Why are you doing this?"

The cultist grinned. "Baal will rise again, and all will succumb to the darkness."

Before Josh could respond, a pitchfork came tearing through the exterior wall and impaled the cultist, whose eyes drifted down to the pointed, blood-and-splinter-covered ends of the pitchfork protruding through his abdomen. Blood spurted from the man's mouth, and he slumped over, dead. Everyone but Josh and Nick screamed.

Without warning, the cabin began to shake. Lightning flashing out-side cast the forest in a haunting glow. Wind rattled the walls with such force that Nick thought the cabin might collapse.

"What's happening?" Reagan shouted over the sound of thunder.

I don't like this. Nick stared at the door. Something bad was coming. He could feel it in his bones.

Josh crossed the room and threw open the door. "You guys better get out here."

Harsh winds picked up piles of fallen leaves with the force of a tor-nado. Nick shielded himself as he and the others made their way outside the cabin.

His eyes widened when he saw the crows. "Oh my God."

There were more than he could count. Black crows, remaining per-fectly still amid the sweeping winds, filled the trees surrounding the cabin. They all stared in the campers' direction, and a cold chill settled in the pit of Nick's stomach. He squeezed the axe tightly in his grip. When he listened closely, he heard whispers coming from the forest.

The crows. That's how the scarecrow knows where we are. "We need to go. Now."

Without warning, the crows turned their heads in unison toward the woods, where a tall figure approached from the shadows. As the group watched in terror, the scarecrow emerged beside the burnt-out campfire and regarded them through its malevolent button eye.

"This way." Josh sprinted toward a dirt trail that led away from the cabin. Nick waited for the others to follow before he took off after them. Behind him, the scarecrow staggered toward the cabin, pulled the pitch-fork from the wooden planks, and returned Nick's gaze. For a moment, he could swear its stitched mouth folded into a sinister grin.

Nick ran as if death itself was chasing after him.

Chapter THIRTEEN

Josh led his friends down the trail. The mountains loomed ever closer as the group made their way farther into the rural Eastern Kentucky landscape. Even after hundreds of years, the rough terrain remained untamed by man. Utter stillness had replaced the rushing wind. Josh, accustomed to city life, found the quiet more unsettling. Other than the monsters stalking them, he and his friends were probably the only people around for miles.

His flashlight's beam wavered. Josh tapped the metal case, and the light glowed brightly once more. They had been walking for at least two miles, and there were still no markers of civilization to indicate that they were any closer to leaving the forest behind. He remembered the nearly endless array of trees on the drive to the campsite. More likely than not, they had a long way yet to go. The feeling wasn't all that different from when they were trapped in the cornfield. But where the cornfield had evoked claustrophobic feelings—he felt suffocated by the maze of tightly packed stalks—the forest was spacious. There was no way to tell what might be hiding just out of sight.

The campers kept close to each other and shined their flashlights into different places in search of anything out of the ordinary. Everyone was careful not to fall too far behind. No one had spoken since leaving the cabin. Josh guessed the others didn't want to risk alerting whatever was out there to their presence. Either that or they were still in denial.

Josh understood that well enough. Everything about the night of his parents' deaths, from the moment he pulled the trigger, was a blur. It was only in his dreams that he was cursed to remember everything. The dreams were preferable to the nightmares where his father wouldn't stay dead. Even with a bullet through his heart, his father's ghost continued to haunt him.

Reagan broke the silence with a string of profanities. "Still no service. I hate this place." She regarded her phone with disgust. She'd been checking the phone regularly for the last half hour. "It doesn't make sense."

"Why not?" Brooke asked. "We probably won't have better reception until we're out of the woods."

"Even with no bars, our phones should still be able to make emergency calls. I've tried several times to send a distress signal without success."

"Maybe this place is so rural even an SOS won't get picked up." Josh glanced at his own phone to check the time. It was just after midnight. That left several hours, trapped inside the forest with the scarecrow and who knew what else lurking in the shadows, until sunrise. "Or maybe the cave system emits some sort of magnetic field that interferes with our signals."

Chad motioned to Reagan to put her phone away. "Either way, can you stop checking your phone every five seconds? That thing will see the light if you're not careful."

Reagan narrowed her gaze at her boyfriend. "Like it won't notice our flashlights?" She shined her light in his face for good measure.

Chad brought up his hands to shield his eyes. "I still can't believe you bailed on me in the truck."

"We've been over this." Reagan scoffed in derision. "Do you really think I was going to sit there and watch while you crashed into the barn? Besides, you did the same thing to Nick."

"You could have come back for me." Chad sounded hurt. "We're supposed to be a team. I protected you from that maniac back there, didn't I?"

"I saved myself. You stumbled onto me by mistake. It was *literally* the least you could do."

"Whatever." Chad threw his hands up in frustration and hobbled away.

On any other night, Josh would have welcomed the strife between his love interest and romantic rival. Unfortunately, it was coming at the very moment they most needed to hang together.

What a nightmare this trip has turned into. He had hoped it would be a time to celebrate the past, and that maybe he and Reagan might officially get together at last. How differently everything had turned out. He couldn't help feeling responsible. After all, the whole thing was his idea.

Josh knew Reagan's attitude was a mask for her fear. She could fool the others in the group, but not him. Allowing Nick to take the lead, he dropped back and walked alongside her. "Are you okay?"

"What do you think?" She hadn't lost the characteristic bluntness that was part of her appeal to him.

Josh studied her in the moonlight. Even with her hair a mess and her face stained with dirt, she was still the most beautiful girl he had ever seen. "Everything's going to be okay. I won't let anything happen to you."

Her expression softened. "I need you, Josh. Chad can't protect me like you can. You're the only one who has a chance of getting us out of here." She slipped her hand into his while they trailed behind the others. The touch of her skin sent a warm feeling rushing through him that even the cold air couldn't dispel.

After his parents died, Josh went to live with his aunt. He didn't know his mother's sister very well before that time, but she lived in Louisville, which meant he didn't have to move to another city and leave his life behind. Even with Brooke to help him through the pain of his loss, for a long time Josh felt like a shadow of the person he used to be. He dealt with his trauma by retreating further into books and his schoolwork. Although he put on a show for Brooke, Josh didn't entertain the possibility of happiness for himself. Then he met Reagan, and everything changed.

That fall, he started making new friends at his new school. Reagan, a sharp-witted girl with an equally sharp tongue in his American Literature class, was one of these friends. Josh was smitten from the moment he saw her. She was beautiful, but she was also the first person he'd met who could challenge him intellectually. When he was with Reagan, he felt like he could drop the mask he'd adopted after his parents' deaths and actually be himself. Against his better judgment, he had fallen in love.

Nick shined his flashlight through a gap in the trees. "What's that ahead?"

The group emerged from the wooded area onto a hill where most of the trees had been cleared away. They weren't truly out of the woods—the forest surrounded the property on all sides—but at least out in the open, they would have an easier time seeing a threat coming their way.

The ground was mostly barren and covered with rocks. Weeds grew over the faint outline of a trail that had probably been abandoned for decades. Josh saw the remains of a sign that warned against trespassing as he slipped through a gateway in a rusty fence bordering the property.

Brooke followed him through the gate. "What is this place?"

Nick trained his flashlight on a set of tracks. "The railroad came through here. We should look around. Maybe there's a radio somewhere."

"Don't go too far," Josh said as the group spread out to explore the location, to remind them to stick together.

He counted four small buildings scattered across the property. Most had withered and rotted with age. One had completely collapsed inward on itself. Josh trained the beam on a smudged window and peered inside. Other than a row of shelves bearing a few cobweb-covered pickaxes, the room was mostly bare.

No one's been here in years. He passed a broken-down wheelbarrow beside the tracks and moved the flashlight beam along the inside of a wooden wagon full of coal.

As the others looked around, Josh silently began piecing together everything that had happened since their arrival. Their conversation inside the cabin shed light on most of the events that had occurred, but not everything. It was clear that something supernatural was going on—scarecrows didn't just get up and walk of their own volition—but that still didn't explain the fact that people had been going missing from the area for years.

Reagan's story about Wyatt, on the other hand, made more sense. Josh suspected the killings were the reason the cult had chosen their location in the first place. From what he heard in the cornfield, and what Reagan learned from Wyatt, the cult believed the caves were a gateway to hell. They claimed killings affected the gateway, which was why the cult was trying to use it to summon a demon.

Somehow, it all went back to the scarecrow. According to what he'd learned on Reddit, all the scarecrows from Gray Hollow were destroyed. Only they hadn't been, because one resurfaced in Booneville two years later. The newspapers never mentioned what became of the scarecrow after that. If Josh's guess was right, the scarecrow stalking them and the scarecrow connected with the Booneville murders were one and the same.

In both cases he read about, the scarecrow had been stopped—but how? Jezebel Woods, the sheriff who was investigating the Gray Hollow murders, had vanished without a trace. Whatever was happening, Josh couldn't escape the feeling it was connected with what occurred in Gray Hollow, but without internet access or cell phone reception, his link to outside information was cut off. There was still too much he didn't know. Josh wasn't sure if they'd survive the night, but he was certain there was more to the cult's plans than even he suspected.

He turned his attention to Nick, only a short distance away. They hadn't shared a moment alone since the madness began. Josh thought again of how Nick had put himself in danger to allow him and Brooke to escape. He approached Nick, who looked back at him in the pale light. "About what I said earlier."

"Don't worry about it. I probably had it coming."

"Maybe I was wrong." Josh took a step closer to his brother. "You have changed."

Something moved in the forest behind them, and Nick swung his flashlight toward the trees. Neither made a sound until a deer bounded away from the light.

Nick returned his gaze to Josh. "I wasn't always a screw-up as a brother, you know. I was a better brother when we were kids."

"No. You were the best."

Nick let out a deep sigh. "I wish there was a good reason why I missed the funeral. The truth was, I was passed out. I spent the night before drinking and crying myself to sleep."

"I guess we both dealt with it in our own ways."

Nick shook his head. "As soon as things got tough, I dove right into the bottle, just like Dad. I should have been strong—like you."

"How did you stop drinking?"

"There was this girl. Her name was Grace."

"I should have known." If not for the gravity of the situation, Josh might have laughed. With Nick, there had always been plenty of girls. He was like Chad in that respect. Even when they were kids, Nick never had any difficulty getting girls to like him.

"This one was different." Nick spoke as if he knew what Josh was thinking. "She wasn't like the others."

"Was?" Josh raised an eyebrow at his brother's curious wording.

Chad's voice echoed across the stillness before Nick could answer. "I think we found the coal mine."

Darkness spilled out of the mine's entrance, partially boarded over with wooden planks nailed across the posts. When Josh fixed his light on a post, he noticed a letter carved into the wood. He moved the beam to reveal a message that had been left behind.

Danger.

Brooke shuddered. "Creepy."

Nick moved to face Reagan. "You said there was a town somewhere around here?"

"It was abandoned when the mine shut down. Wyatt said the Native Americans that lived here believed something evil had taken root in the cave."

Chad regarded the vast darkness beyond the beam. "Well, we're definitely not going in there. Any other ideas?"

"There." Josh pointed to a watchtower higher up the mountain. At one time, an overseer would have supervised the functioning of the mine from the vantage point it provided. "That should give us a better look at what's in the valley below. Maybe we'll get a glimpse of the road."

Chad directed his flashlight toward the platform, and the beam fell on a decaying wooden ladder that led to the top. "There's no way those steps will hold our weight."

Reagan nodded vigorously. "Agreed. Someone should go up there alone while the rest of us keep watch down here."

"What about you, Reagan?" Nick asked. She was the smallest.

Reagan looked at Nick as if he'd gone mad. "And risk falling through the rotten planks? Forget it. I'm not going up there, alone or otherwise."

"I'll do it," Brooke volunteered.

"Thanks." Josh squeezed her arm before she started up the hill, and Brooke offered a brave smile.

He watched anxiously as she made the climb up the ladder. Brooke slipped just before she reached the top, and Josh found himself holding his breath at the possibility she might fall. She held onto the rung above her and hauled herself onto the platform, and he let out a sigh of relief.

It's a good thing we sent an athlete up there.

"Can you see anything?" Chad called to her.

Brooke peered from the platform. "I don't know. It's so dark." She swept her flashlight over the area below. "I can't see any sign of the road from here."

"Anything else?" Josh did his best to hide his disappointment.

Brooke didn't answer for a moment. "I think there are buildings in the valley—it could be the town."

"Do you see anything beyond that?"

"Nothing. Just fog. There's mist everywhere."

Nick claimed Bartholomew had used witchcraft to conjure the mist and trap them inside the forest. If true, no how matter how far they ran, they were stuck until dawn, and that was something Josh couldn't accept. There had to be a way out. He just needed to find it. Otherwise, everything would be in vain.

Josh beckoned for Brooke to come down. "We have to keep going. We'll head for what's left of the town and see what else we can find." At the moment, it was all they could do, while hoping the scarecrow didn't find them in the meantime.

As Brooke switched off her flashlight and started toward the ladder, a gunshot rang out. When the bullet struck the watchtower, Brooke fell backward, and the flashlight plunged over the edge.

"Brooke!" Hoping the bullet hadn't found its mark, Josh scrambled to help.

"Wait!" Nick stretched out his hand in warning moments before another bullet ripped into the rocks beside Josh.

The night erupted into chaos. Josh, powerless to help Brooke—who was dangling from the platform in a desperate attempt to hold on—dived behind the collapsed building for cover. He glanced back and saw Chad and Reagan hide near the mineshaft. Nick crouched a few feet away beside the railroad tracks.

"Help!" Brooke screamed. Another bullet hit the platform.

Josh spotted a gleam of light in the trees, where a tall figure loomed. *Wyatt.* When the killer stopped to reload his gun, Josh threw himself forward to distract Wyatt and give Brooke the chance to escape. The closer he got, the clearer the figure's features became. Long black hair framed an evil face and eyes that seemed to glow in the moonlight. When he saw Josh coming, Wyatt pointed the gun at him, but it was too late to turn back. Josh made final eye contact with Brooke, who had pulled herself over the edge, and braced himself for the end.

Nick tackled Josh from behind as the gunshot echoed through the air, and they fell under the bushes.

"What are you doing?" Josh tried to get to his feet, but Nick held him pinned to the ground and covered him with his body.

The rifle sounded several times in rapid succession and sprayed bullets around them. Josh felt Nick's body jerk twice over him, and a long silence fell over the property.

"Nick?" Josh prodded his brother. "Are you okay?"

Nick didn't answer. Josh felt something warm and wet dripping onto his back. He rolled Nick off his body and saw blood in the moonlight.

Chapter FOURTEEN

12:47 A.M.

The last rung broke under her feet. Brooke hit the hard ground and rolled downhill. She was banged up but not seriously injured. The rifle had fallen still, at least for the moment. She searched for Josh, Nick, or Wyatt. Without her flashlight, lost to the darkness, there was only the moonlight to guide her.

Josh had put himself in harm's way to save her—again. Brooke was tired of everyone having to come to her rescue, but most of all, she was tired of being afraid. She had always been afraid. She was afraid that her mother wouldn't be able to function without her help. She was afraid to tell Josh how she felt. Now, caught in a life-or-death scenario, the things that once frightened her paled in comparison.

Reagan's voice was audible amid the sounds emitted by the nocturnal animals. "We need to get out of here."

Brooke craned her neck and saw Reagan and Chad hunched beside the mineshaft.

"What about the others?" Chad's outline was barely visible in the moonlight.

"It's too late for them," Reagan said. "You're the only one who can get us to safety. Please, Chad. What if Wyatt comes back?"

For a moment, everything was quiet. Then Brooke heard Chad's voice. "Okay. Stay here—I'll scout ahead to make sure he's gone."

Brooke was about to let them know she was still breathing when she heard footsteps.

Wyatt. Brooke quietly crawled behind a pile of rocks and hoped he wouldn't notice her.

When he had chased her through the woods earlier, he was too far away to get a good look at him. Now she saw his towering figure up close, and he was terrifying to behold. In his own way, he was almost as horrible to look at as the scarecrow. He carried a metal chain in bloodstained hands and walked with a slight hunch.

Fortunately, despite their proximity, Wyatt's attention was elsewhere. A set of monstrous yellow teeth gleamed in his mouth as he called down the mountain. "I know you're down there."

From her vantage point, Brooke saw Chad—exposed in the open—freeze while Reagan remained hidden at the mineshaft. Chad quickly darted behind one of the abandoned buildings, but not before Wyatt noticed him.

"I hope you didn't think you could get away from me, Reagan." Wyatt made a beeline toward the spot where Chad was hiding. "There's still so much I want to show you." He made a show of searching in the darkness. "Thanks for bringing your friends. I told you I'd let you watch them die."

Chad showed no signs of budging. Was he unaware that Wyatt was closing in on him?

Move. Brooke told herself to be strong and picked up a pickaxe that had long ago been discarded. As she crept closer, she watched the scene unfold like something out of a horror movie. Wyatt's shadow fell over Chad, who noticed the killer too late. Before he could flee, Wyatt hit him hard enough with the chain to knock him to the ground. When Wyatt raised the chain again, Brooke swung the pickaxe at him and struck him in the side. The aged tool broke in her hands and left her holding the useless end.

Wyatt turned to face her. "Hello again."

Brooke expected Chad to help, but he scrambled to his feet and sprinted toward the woods. She cast her gaze toward the mineshaft, where Reagan had similarly disappeared.

Wyatt twirled the chain in a deadly motion. "It looks like it's just the two of us. Some friends you've got."

Left with no other option, Brooke fled into the mine with the killer trailing behind.

Reagan did her best to keep from slipping while running downhill. She didn't know where the others were, and she didn't care. All that mattered was that the danger was behind her.

This isn't happening. It couldn't be. Demons and scarecrows and cults—these things just didn't happen, not in the real world. Yet here she was with her world falling apart at the seams. The likeliest possibility was that it was *all* a delusion, but that was the possibility she was most afraid of.

It was her secret fear, one she never mentioned aloud. Reagan kept her mother's diagnosis from everyone. It wasn't that she was embarrassed. There was something intensely vulnerable about sharing the truth, and she had vowed never to be vulnerable again.

Reagan had visited her mother once, when she was thirteen years old. None of her foster parents had allowed Reagan to see her. At the time, she hadn't laid eyes on her mother in the five years since she was committed. After she was finally adopted, Reagan succeeded in gaining permission to visit Central State Hospital, Kentucky's primary long-term psychiatric facility.

Josh had told her once about studies demonstrating that patients with severe schizophrenia had brain scan results mirroring changes seen in Alzheimer's disease. With each psychotic episode, the patient moved further from their original baseline, until at last they no longer resembled the person they once were. Reagan believed him.

Nothing could have prepared her for what she encountered in that hospital. Whoever it was, it wasn't her mother. The change in her mother's physical appearance was staggering. It was as if she had aged twenty years in five. Her hair was wild and unruly, and her face was pale and gaunt. She seemed to see without really seeing.

Reagan never visited her mother again. After that visit, she shed the last vestige of the girl she was before her mother's diagnosis, but no matter how hard she tried to turn the page, she could never fully forget the image of her mother. That was her private terror. There was a strong genetic component to schizophrenia, a disease that usually manifested in an individual's twenties or early thirties. Reagan lived with the fear she might one day develop the disorder, and everything she was would be taken away again. Given all that she had experienced since their arrival at the campsite, she was beginning to wonder if it hadn't happened already.

Briars tore into her legs and cut her skin. Reagan let out a cry of anguish and looked back over her shoulder just to make sure Wyatt hadn't followed her. The outline of the mining property was only faintly visible through the trees. She heard leaves crunching below, where a faint mist rose higher up the mountain.

"Chad?" She peered into the mist, and for a moment she thought she saw a shadowy figure across from her. Reagan trained her flashlight on the area, but there was nothing there. With a shaking hand, she pulled out her cell phone and checked again for reception. *No luck.*

When she lowered the phone, the scarecrow stood directly in front of her.

Reagan tumbled backward, and the phone slipped out of her hand and into the darkness. Before her attacker could lift its pitchfork to stab her, she pointed the flashlight at it, and the scarecrow recoiled from the light.

Pinned between the scarecrow at her back and the killer above, Reagan pushed herself up and retreated the way she came.

Chad ran as fast as his mangled ankle allowed. Fear helped him push through the pain. The sound of screams remained audible behind him while he hurried away from the mine. He couldn't help looking back, but he was too far away to see the mine through the trees. He forced himself to ignore Brooke's screams and keep going.

He pictured the look on her face when he abandoned her and felt a sudden flare of shame. She'd risked everything to help him, just as Nick had earlier. How had he returned the favor? By leaving them to die. He'd taken the easy way out again, as he had so many times before. It was more than selfish—it was cowardly.

Chad's father always said he wasn't good enough. His father was a self-made businessman, rich and successful. When Chad was younger, he tried desperately to please the old man, but nothing was ever good enough. Everything had to be done exactly his father's way. Even when

Chad tried his best, his father always found fault with something. He was almost relieved when his parents divorced. At least his stepdad treated him like a real person.

Eventually, Chad gave up trying to please his father and decided not to worry about what he or anyone else thought. There was no point in trying if he was doomed to fail eventually, so why not take the easy way out? On the surface, he had everything going for him. He was a star athlete from a wealthy home and he was dating the girl of his dreams. Deep down, however, Chad knew it wouldn't last. Despite his talent, he wasn't gifted enough to play football at the college level. With his grades as poor as they were, he doubted there was a future for him in higher education.

The truth was, this was as good as his life was ever going to be. After high school, the façade would come crumbling down around him. Reagan was already pulling away. He had always been little more than arm candy to her, but he went along with it because of how strongly he felt about her. As he hurried through the brush, Chad couldn't help recalling how easily she left him before. Here he was, doing the very same thing. He had always been a disappointment, to Reagan and his father alike. Most of all, he was disappointed in himself.

The screams faded, and Chad thought he saw something that looked like the road beyond the fog rising across the valley. He stopped and stared into the mist. When he looked back over his shoulder, his hands balled into fists.

Not this time.

He turned around and sprinted back toward the mines while crows flocked at his back. Maybe he wasn't too late.

Bartholomew knelt in the center of the cornfield and faced the altar. With his eyes closed, he stretched out his hands to the darkness and became one with the endless night. Through his possession of the crows, he observed each of the campers' pitiful attempts to save themselves. They could not hide from him.

The wind stirred behind him, and he sensed a presence approaching through the cornfield. "Do not enter the circle."

The hooded figure at his back glanced down at her feet, dangerously close to the circle around the altar. She took a step back and waited at the stalks' edge. "Forgive me, master."

"Why have you come, Rebecca?" His back remained to her.

The old woman lowered her hood. "We searched the cabin. The offerings were gone."

"Do you think I did not already know?" He felt a tinge of irritation that she had interrupted his trance over such a trivial matter.

"Three of our members have been killed."

"We are not the only ones stalking the forest this night." The gunman was an unforeseen wrinkle in his plans, but perhaps one that could be turned to his advantage.

"The scarecrow murdered one."

Bartholomew slowly rose and turned to face her. "More will die until the ritual is complete." He approached the edge of the circle until only the line was between them. "You failed to tell me about the girl's companions."

She flinched from his gaze. "It was an oversight. I apologize."

"That oversight has cost us dearly. I am beginning to regret giving you authority over this sect. Do you have any idea how long I've prepared for this night? This ritual must succeed."

"Did we not secure the scarecrow from Booneville? We recovered it from the barn and repaired it as you instructed, and it was I who administered the drugged tea to the girl."

Underneath the skull, his face contorted with rage. He had given her a share of power, and she had grown arrogant. "You forget where your power comes from. It is my blood that has prolonged your life. Your brethren in Gray Hollow would have succeeded by now." Before she could react, Bartholomew grabbed her by the throat. "If you cannot handle a group of mere adolescents, what use are you to me?"

"Forgive me. We will locate them."

He released her, and she fell to the ground at his feet. "You will find them at the mines, on their way to the abandoned settlement. Do not fail me again."

The old woman retreated into the stalks, and Bartholomew returned to the altar.

Soon. It was almost time.

Chapter FIFTEEN

1:31 A.M.

Reagan had never been more afraid in all her life. She thought she could escape the madness by allowing Brooke to draw Wyatt's attention away from her. Instead, she had run head-first into an even greater evil.

Adrenaline roused by the walking nightmare at her back surged through her veins like an electric shock. Her heart beat so fast the rhythm was nearly a continuous dance. Reagan tripped over a rock, lost her balance, and landed in a briar patch. Her flashlight rolled just out of reach. She stifled a scream from briars tearing into her skin and groped for the flashlight.

Something loomed behind her. Reagan let out a whimper and looked over her shoulder. The scarecrow's stitched smile looked back at her, and she trembled. The scarecrow grabbed her ankle and pulled her through the dry leaves, but Reagan kicked free and lunged for the flashlight. Her hand closed around the cold metal just in time, and the beam exploded into the night. Reagan pointed the flashlight into the thing's face.

Shrieking, the scarecrow shielded itself from the light. Reagan, unable to look away from the scarecrow's burlap face, crawled along the ground through the briars. She grabbed a tree to steady herself, but the scarecrow hurled the pitchfork in her direction, and the spikes hit the tree with a twang, mere inches from her face.

Reagan was on her feet in an instant. She held onto the flashlight for dear life and tore back up the mountain. Below, the scarecrow yanked the pitchfork from the tree. Although she did her best to quicken her pace, every time Reagan looked back, the scarecrow was even closer. How was that possible? When she had first glimpsed the scarecrow at the cabin, it lumbered slowly with a shuffling gait. Now, it was running. Was the scarecrow actually getting stronger?

It still doesn't like the light. Something had burned it before. That meant it could be hurt.

Footsteps approached across the dry leaves, and a withered hand grabbed at her shoulder. Reagan stumbled but kept going. Despite the burning in her legs from the steep incline, she pushed herself harder. The hilltop loomed above, just out of reach. Mist rising at her ankles ensnared everything in its path. As she neared the top, she noticed the footsteps had faded. When she looked back, the scarecrow was gone.

Reagan let out a sigh of relief. The rusted fence lining the mining property was visible farther up the mountain. She started to shout for help in hopes one of the others would hear her and come to the rescue, but she had left them behind. If anyone heard her, it was likely to be Wyatt.

Her gaze fell on a path she hoped would lead to the abandoned town Brooke had spotted from the watchtower. Before she took another step, something moved at her back. Reagan spun around and held her flashlight on the bushes, where something stirred again. She stepped forward cautiously and kept the beam of light on the rustling leaves. A flock of crows swarmed out of the bushes and sent her sprawling backward. The mist surrounded her as she hit her head on the ground, and the flashlight shattered against a rock.

Reagan moaned and rolled over. Her vision blurred, and she perceived two pairs of boots approaching through the fog. The scarecrow's face, upside down, leaped out at her from the dark. As it reached for her, she swung the broken flashlight at its head as hard as she could. Her head still spinning, she did her best to stand and started toward the path with the scarecrow following close behind.

Nick had gone to college to escape an abusive home. He certainly didn't go to fall in love.

Nick had always been popular. It was true in high school and even more so in college. He didn't have any trouble making friends or meeting girls. None of them ever really meant anything to him, though; he'd learned his parents' lesson a little too well. It was better not to care about anyone but himself.

It hadn't taken him long to discover the bottle. Despite his disgust with his father, Nick fell easily into the same trap. He lived for college parties—for any time when he didn't have to feel pain. It didn't matter if it was the weekend or a school night. He stopped going to class. His grades declined.

He met Grace the semester before he flunked out. It was easy to see that she was sick. The oxygen tank made that clear enough. She was pale, as if she hardly spent any time in the sun. Her raven-black hair, falling almost to her waist, only heightened the stark colorlessness of her skin. She was small and impossibly thin, and yet there was somehow nothing fragile about her.

Nick was on his way to a fraternity house at the end of the block when she coughed and waved to him.

"Is something wrong?"

"You wouldn't mind giving me a ride to the clinic, would you?" She held up the oxygen tank and smiled widely. "I'm not feeling too hot, and my car just decided to die on me."

"Actually, I was on my way to a party," Nick had replied. "Do we know each other?"

She thrust her hand at him. "I'm Grace."

He shook her hand somewhat reluctantly. "Nick."

"Now that we know each other, I was hoping you would be my Good Samaritan."

Nick looked at her for a long moment and sighed. "Fine."

Once inside his car, they sat quietly for a few awkward moments before Grace broke the silence. "So, what's your major?"

"Biology."

Her eyes danced. "Really? Mine too!" Her excitement faded. "Why haven't I seen you in any classes?"

Nick grinned. "I don't spend too much time in class."

"That doesn't sound like a recipe for success."

"Look, I'm not in the business of judging *you*. Besides, I didn't see anyone else offering you a ride."

She held up her hands in mock surrender. "I meant no offense. So, why biology?"

"I never really gave it much thought. I guess I really just wanted to get away from home."

"Me too. My parents thought I would be too sick to go away to school. It took me forever to convince them to let me leave home. What about you?"

"It's a family thing," he said in a tone that implied he'd rather not discuss it. "What kind of sickness do you have, anyway? Aren't you a little young for an oxygen tank?"

"I have cystic fibrosis. It's a fancy way of saying my lungs don't work right." Grace coughed again and stopped talking. It looked like she was struggling to breathe, and Nick pressed on the gas a little harder.

He stayed with her at the hospital while she waited for her parents to arrive from out of town. She told him he could leave, but Nick couldn't help feeling if it were him, he wouldn't want to be alone in a hospital. Besides, even though she seemed sort of strange, he enjoyed talking to her.

Finally, she received a text that her parents had arrived, and Nick got up to go. "Guess I'll see you around." He privately doubted it.

"Hey, Nick," she called as he approached the door.

"Yeah?"

"You're a better guy than you give yourself credit for."

As he lay atop the mountain, Nick could almost hear her speaking to him in the dark. "Grace?"

"It's me—it's Josh."

When Nick opened his eyes, he found himself looking up at his younger brother. "What happened?"

"You saved me. You shielded me with your body. Are you okay?"

Nick moaned and sat up. "I'll live, but I feel like I've been kicked in the head by a horse." He put his hand to the back of his head and felt blood.

"You got lucky. The bullet only grazed you."

"Luck had nothing to do with it."

Grace's words came back to him from the past. "God still has a plan for you, Nick."

"Someone was looking out for me." *He's not finished with me yet.* When Nick tried to stand, his leg throbbed with burning pain. His pant leg was stained with more blood. "I think I caught another bullet in the leg. Some trip, huh? Just look at us—one shot, one stabbed."

"We've been through worse." Josh extended a hand to help Nick up. "You saved my life, Nick."

"That's what brothers are for." Nick leaned on him for support until he was able to walk on his own. "I don't hear gunshots." Silence had settled over the property.

Josh cast a furtive glance up the mountain. "I think he's gone."

"Are you sure?"

Even in the moonlight, it was nearly impossible to see into the shadows. If Wyatt were still hiding nearby, turning on the flashlight would only risk giving away their position. Josh slipped out of sight, and Nick found himself growing uneasy until his brother returned moments later.

"Well? What did you see?"

Josh shook his head. "Nothing."

Nick hesitated. "What happened to the others?"

It was clear from Josh's expression he didn't know the answer. Before either could speak, a scream rang out from below.

Josh's eyes widened with realization. "Brooke."

Nick gritted his teeth and picked up the fallen axe he'd dropped when he tackled Josh. "Come on."

The brothers raced downhill, ready to confront whatever awaited them in the night below—together.

Brooke ducked under the wooden beams meant to bar her passage farther into the mine. Wyatt's shadow fell over the entrance, and Brooke, enveloped by darkness, stumbled forward. The moonlight outside the mine grew fainter with every step she took until at last the cavern devoured the light.

Brooke reached into her pocket and took out her cell phone. The phone's flashlight was far weaker than the one she'd lost, but it was the only light source she had left. She shuddered from a rush of cool air. The mine was cold and damp. Water trickled softly somewhere in the shadows. Each drop fell to the ground with near-perfect regularity.

Brooke advanced cautiously and tried her best to make out her surroundings in the faint illumination. She encountered a fork in the passage but kept to the path she was on. Even if she could no longer hear him, she was certain Wyatt had followed her into the mine. Brooke peered into the darkness ahead. How deep exactly did the mine go? It was almost impossible to see more than a few feet ahead, and she didn't want to risk stepping over a ledge and falling to her death.

The phone's light washed over a sign nailed to a support beam.

Warning, the sign read. *Shaft unstable.* She didn't want to think about the possibility of the mine collapsing around her.

Brooke quickened her pace and nearly ran face-first into a low-hanging support beam. She ducked under it at the last second and barely managed to keep her footing on the slick floor. The mineshaft's walls were wet with condensation that shimmered under the phone's light.

Wyatt's voice reverberated from the mine's walls. "I'm going to eat you alive."

How is he able to see in here without a flashlight? Brooke hoped she was too far ahead for him to follow her light. *Be brave.* Wyatt wanted her to panic and lose her calm, but she didn't plan to give him the satisfaction. By leading him farther into the mine, she was keeping him away from the others.

Ahead, something was painted across one of the rock walls. Brooke approached, momentarily transfixed, and ran her hand over the stone surface. What appeared to be Native American symbols depicted a black sun over a mountain. Painted crows flocked over the mountain. As she stepped back to take in the whole image, she saw dozens of stick figures sprawled under the mountain in what appeared to be blood. The phone wavered in her hand.

Brooke wondered how long ago the symbols were left there. She supposed they predated the cult's existence on the mountain by many years. The Natives must have known there was something evil living in the system of caves within the mountains. Brooke wondered if any remnant of the tribe still existed in the area, or if they had died out. Either way, she guessed they left the symbols as a warning for others, which the miners evidently had ignored. From the scarecrow to the cult and even Wyatt, the presence that resided inside the cave was responsible for it all. That was why the cult tried to sacrifice her—to bring it back through the gateway.

Without warning, the flashlight shut off, and the cave went dark around her. *Less than ten percent battery left,* warned a message from her cell phone, and Brooke's heart skipped a beat. What if the cell phone ran out of battery before she returned to the surface? She'd never be able to find her way back to the mine's entrance without light.

She moved her finger to dismiss the message and turn the flashlight on again, but at that moment she heard footsteps nearby. Wyatt was close—she could feel it. Brooke spotted a narrow cranny in the wall in the dim glow of her phone's screen. She squeezed through the crack into an adjoining chamber and waited as the footsteps grew louder. Brooke coughed on a lungful of dusty air, and the footsteps stopped. She squatted low on the ground and prayed Wyatt hadn't heard her.

"Come out, little girl. I know you're close. I can hear your heart beating." For a moment, all fell quiet, and Brooke let out a sigh of relief. Then his voice became a deafening roar. "I'm going to cut it out!"

Shaking, she took a step back, and her foot landed in a puddle of something wet. The consistency felt thick, like tar. Unable to see clearly in the dark, Brooke was about to dip her finger in the substance, but at that moment, more voices rang out through the cave.

"Brooke! Are you in there?"

Nick and Josh. Brooke peered through the split in the wall and saw beams of light from their flashlights coming from the mine's entrance. Their flashlights unmasked a shadowy figure on the other side of the cranny. Wyatt had been there the whole time, waiting for her to give herself away. Brooke clamped a hand over her mouth and watched as he slipped beyond the illumination's reach and followed the source of the light.

When she was sure he was gone, Brooke flipped on her phone's flashlight function. Light flooding through the chamber uncovered a massive break in the wall behind her. Brooke stiffened. It was the entrance to the underground cave system the miners had discovered so long ago. There were thick puddles of a black, viscous substance everywhere, just like the one she nearly touched moments ago. The tarry substance dripped from the ceiling, clung to the walls, and collected in puddles along the floor. Shadows seemed to rise from the tar to reach out toward the light like claws. Brooke stared into the gaping hole in the cavern wall, where a faint light glowed deeper within the cave. Entranced, she started forward. The light was like fire, but an even deeper red.

Just before she crossed the threshold, she heard Josh's voice call out to her again. Brooke snapped out of the trance and forced herself to look away from the light. When she glanced down, the flashlight gave form to a precipitous drop into the cave's bowels. She trembled at how close she had come to stepping over the edge.

Brooke took a sharp breath and held it as she ran back the way she came, hoping Wyatt wasn't lurking in the shadows. She listened for Josh and Nick, but their voices had already faded. Her phone's battery was almost down to one percent. Just before the light shut off, she saw the blood moon's pale glow outside the mine's entrance. There were flashlights ahead, and she could barely make out two figures through the night. She scanned the area she could see from the cave's mouth for Wyatt.

"I thought you'd go running after them." Wyatt grabbed her from behind and threw her into the safety beams nailed across the entrance. The beams splintered under her weight, and the collision knocked the air out of her lungs. She hit the ground hard.

She saw the flashlights shine in her direction. Brooke scrambled to her feet, but Wyatt swung the chain and knocked her down again. She watched helplessly as he pulled a hunting knife from its sheath and held it over her.

Josh slammed into Wyatt, who absorbed the weight of the impact unharmed and batted Josh to the ground with a single blow. Nick swung his axe at Wyatt, but Wyatt caught the axe's handle and head-butted Nick, and the axe clattered out of reach.

"Which one of you do I kill first?" Wyatt pointed the knife at each one of them in turn before training it on Brooke.

She pushed herself up and met his eyes. "Come and get me."

He took a step in her direction, and Brooke ran as fast as she could for the fence in hopes of leading him away from her friends. As she slid under the bottom rung, Wyatt charged her like a bull, and she threw herself out of the way, lost her balance, and rolled downhill. She landed in a creek. The frigid water drenched her clothes, and when she tried to stand, she slipped and fell.

Wyatt, looming over her, blotted out the moon. He raised the heavy chain and spun it in the air. "Game over."

With a heroic shout, Chad emerged from the brush and brandished Nick's fallen axe. Wyatt reacted a half-second too late, and the axe plunged into his back. The killer stared at Chad for a long moment before tearing the axe free from his back and casting it into the creek.

Chad's eyes widened in surprise and the triumphant expression vanished from his face as quickly as it had appeared. "Get out of here, Brooke."

Someone grabbed Brooke's hand and pulled her into the brush. She started to scream, but a hand clamped over her mouth. She heard Josh say, "It's okay. It's just us."

Nick crouched beside him. Blood stained his clothes all over.

"Chad came back for me. We have to help him." Brooke watched through the bushes as Wyatt struck Chad in the face. Chad's knees buckled, and he went out like a light. Wyatt looked back at the spot where they were hidden before picking Chad up and slinging him over his shoulder.

Before anyone could move to follow them, Reagan sprinted from the trees.

"Reagan?" Josh's gaze narrowed in her direction. "What's wrong?"

She ran past them without a word.

Behind her, the scarecrow stepped into the moonlight.

Chapter SIXTEEN

Wyatt had almost disappeared into the trees with Chad's unconscious form slung over his back. The scarecrow, barely visible through the storm of crows, fixed its attention on Nick, as if singling him out from the others. Nick's hands balled into fists at his sides, and he turned to face the monster. He was tired of running.

Josh yelled his name, and Nick cast a final glance in Chad's direction. He was gone. It was another reminder that he couldn't save everyone—just like he couldn't save Grace. That didn't mean he couldn't try.

We'll come back for you. Ignoring the pain in his leg, Nick bounded after the others before the cloud of crows could envelop him.

Grace hadn't given up, not even when her lungs were closing and she struggled to breathe. She had always carried her light into the darkness. Even now, he could feel it with him. Nick wasn't going to give up either—no matter what.

The birds tore into him. The attack nearly knocked him off his feet, but he kept going. He shouted to warn the others of the approaching swarm. Moments before the crows descended and the mist closed in around him, Josh reached back for him. Nick grabbed his brother's outstretched hand and didn't let go.

Josh pulled Nick along, and they took cover under the trees until the swarm lifted and the cawing grew distant.

"I can hardly see anything." Nick peered through the fog. "Are you guys here?"

"I'm here," Brooke said.

"Me too," Reagan replied.

"Hang on." Josh toggled on his flashlight and used its illumination to pierce the fog.

"Where are we?" Nick stopped to make sure his flashlight was in working order before adding its light to Josh's.

"I don't know. Everything happened so fast."

Reagan beckoned to them. "This way. The fog is thinner over there."

They walked to a spot where receding fog permitted a glimpse of the land below. The faint outline of the abandoned town was visible in the flashlight's pale glow.

Reagan groaned. "Finally. There *has* to be a road nearby."

Brooke interrupted. "What about Chad? We can't leave him alone with that psychopath. We have to go back for him."

"Are you crazy?" Reagan shot Brooke a withering look. "What do you think Wyatt will do if he catches us? Besides, we couldn't follow them even if we wanted to—not in this fog."

Nick wasn't so sure. "I saw where they were going. If we retrace our path to the mine, I think we can head in that direction."

"You can't be serious." Reagan looked to Josh for support and found none.

"We can't leave anyone behind."

Before she could reply, wind swept through the trees, and footsteps rustled the dry leaves. Nick swung his beam in the opposite direction, but the space was empty. Even with the flashlight, it was almost impossible to see far in the mist.

Without warning, the pitchfork came sailing out of the fog and missed Nick by a hair's breadth. When he pointed his beam toward the scarecrow, it had vanished again.

Josh took a step back. "Stay together."

The scarecrow materialized at his back. Nick tried to warn him, but Josh reacted too slowly, and the scarecrow pulled him into the fog. Before the mist claimed him, Josh wrenched the knife free from his belt and plunged it into the spot where the scarecrow's heart should have been. Josh forced the knife downward, and ash poured from a tear the length of the scarecrow's chest.

The scarecrow looked down at the gaping hole in its chest and let out a shriek. Its movements became less human and more insect-like as it thrashed in place while trying to pull the knife from its chest. An erratic, jerking limb movement caught Josh in the chest, and he landed on his backside. When the knife clattered to the ground, the scarecrow straightened its back and advanced toward Josh. Nick trained his beam on the scarecrow, and Brooke retrieved Josh's fallen flashlight and did the same. The scarecrow, seemingly wounded by its injury, shrieked and shied away from the light.

"Come on." Nick helped Josh to his feet. "This way."

The group ran together through the fog as the scarecrow faded behind them.

Chad moaned. He had a splitting headache—probably the result of a concussion. He opened his mouth to call out to his coach when he realized he wasn't wearing his football helmet or pads. He blinked a few times and realized that he was slumped over in a chair. A metal chain holding him in place prevented him from moving his arms and legs.

Where am I? As his mind cleared and his eyes adjusted to the dark, the nightmare came rushing back.

He was in a barn. A fire, its warmth a reprieve from the night air, burned in a barrel a short distance away. Soft moonlight seeped into the building through holes in the planks making up the barn's walls.

Where is everyone? The others were gone. As far as he could tell, he wasn't anywhere near the mines. Chad last remembered his encounter with Wyatt before everything had gone black. He hadn't ended up tied to a chair by accident.

He struggled against the restraints, but it was no use. "Help!"

A voice answered him from the dark. "It's just you and me, boy." A massive figure lingered in the shadows. "No one's going to find you out here." Wyatt stepped into the moonlight. His overalls were stained with blood where Chad had struck him with the axe.

Chad's hands trembled involuntarily behind his back. "What do you want from me?"

Wyatt circled the chair like a shark toying with its prey. He leaned closer, and his unpleasant odor made Chad want to gag. "Your life, of course—but first, I want to have a little fun."

"You're sick. Deranged."

Wyatt rounded the chair and hit him in the stomach. The blow knocked the air from his lungs. Before Chad could suck in another breath, Wyatt hit him again and a third time in rapid succession.

"That's twice you've come between me and mine. I wouldn't have pegged you for the heroic type. I can always tell a coward when I see one." Wyatt hit him in the face, and Chad tasted blood.

"Screw you."

Wyatt approached a workbench, where firelight reflected off various scary-looking tools. "Reagan offered me a deal. She said she would help me find the rest of you if I let her go." He lifted a hammer off the table before setting it back down, as if debating his selection. "I'll offer you the same bargain. I've been hunting your friends, but I can't seem to find them. Where were they headed?"

Chad clenched his teeth. For the first time in his life, he had done something truly heroic. He had saved Brooke—and quite possibly the others—by confronting Wyatt. Now the killer was asking him to betray them. "I'm not telling you anything."

Wyatt turned away from the table, and the mocking smile vanished from his face. He grabbed Chad by his hair and jerked his head up until their eyes met. "Pretty boys like you always talk."

They emerged in a forest glade not far from the mine. A creek bathed in the full moon's light trickled softly nearby. Nick surveyed the area while the others stopped to catch their breath. Although the mist had receded, it continued to cling to the hills beneath them.

"Did we lose it?" Brooke followed the beam with her gaze.

Nick nodded. "For now." The scarecrow wasn't going to stop until they were dead. At the moment, however, there were other concerns.

"Look." Josh shined his light on a path that led into the valley below. "I think this trail will lead us into town."

"Then what are we waiting for?" Reagan tugged at Josh's sleeve. "Let's go before the scarecrow comes back."

"We can't leave Chad."

"This again?" Reagan rolled her eyes. "Could you be any more naïve, Brooke? Let me spell it out for you, since you're clearly too dense or too willfully blind to see it for yourself. Chad is dead, and if we try to look for him, we'll just end up lost. Then we'll never find the way out of here."

"Hold on." Nick inspected the earth. "Look." The beam uncovered a set of large footprints leading deeper into the woods. "I'm betting Wyatt left these tracks. They went this way."

"You're as bad as she is!" Reagan threw up her arms in exasperation. "I swear, does anyone want to make it out alive? Josh, talk some sense into them."

Josh, clearly torn, looked from Reagan to Brooke and back again.

Suddenly, a cry echoed through the woods.

"That sounded like Chad." Nick started in the sound's direction without further debate. Brooke and Josh, reluctantly accompanied by Reagan, followed behind. A barn appeared through the brush, and Nick switched off his flashlight and knelt low to peer through the bushes. "Do you hear that? Voices."

He crept through the forest for a better look and glimpsed two figures through the open barn doors. Wyatt had his back to them, while Chad was bound to a chair.

Brooke held a hand over her mouth as Wyatt beat Chad. "We have to do something."

Chad felt his nose break at the next blow. Blood gushed down his face. His left eye had already started to swell shut. Chad spit the blood out of his mouth, and a tooth landed on the floor.

Wyatt gripped his chin in one hand and squeezed. "I can do this all night. Tell me where your friends are while you still have some teeth left."

Chad glared at him but said nothing.

"Have it your way." Wyatt snatched a brand out of the fire and held it inches from his face. "Last chance."

Chad bowed his head in defeat. "Okay. I'll do whatever you want. Just don't hurt me anymore."

"Smart boy. Tell me what I want to know and I'll make it quick and easy."

Chad spoke softly. When Wyatt leaned in to hear him, Chad bit off part of the killer's ear. Wyatt's eyes narrowed in fury, and he ripped open Chad's shirt and thrust the brand below his shoulder blade. Steam rose from the end of the hot iron as his skin sizzled and popped under the intense heat, and Chad nearly blacked out from the searing pain. His eyes burned with tears.

"The others left you to die. Why are you protecting them?" Wyatt returned the brand to the fire. "Don't you want this to stop?"

Chad struggled to hold onto consciousness. His entire body hurt. It would be so easy to give in now. Wyatt was going to kill him anyway. Why not end the suffering? Then Chad thought of Brooke coming to his aid and of how Nick had patched up his leg. "Because they're my friends."

Wyatt returned to the bench and reached for the hammer. "Then I guess we'll have to find out what you value most—your friends or your fingers."

The killer seized Chad's index finger and raised the hammer, and Chad saw movement out of the corner of his eye. When Wyatt followed his gaze, Nick came hurtling out of the darkness and hit him from behind. Wyatt let go of Chad's finger and stumbled back while swinging the hammer blindly. Josh ran at him from the other side and stabbed him in the back with a knife. When Wyatt spun to face Josh, Reagan tossed a rock that hit him in the head.

"Hold on." Brooke appeared beside Chad and worked to free him from the chain.

Chad offered a weak smile "You came back."

"Of course we did. We're all in this together." The chain slid to the ground, and Brooke helped him out of the chair. "Some vacation, right?"

Across the room, Wyatt tossed Nick into the bench, overturning the table in the process. Josh ran at him again, swinging the knife, and the killer caught his wrist and forced the blade back toward Josh's face. Brooke threw herself on Wyatt's back to drag him down, and Chad tackled him and wrapped the chain around Wyatt's neck. Wyatt tried furiously to shake him loose, but Chad hung on and pulled the chain tighter.

Josh, Nick, Brooke, and Reagan took turns beating the killer with whatever they could find. Wyatt's movements slowed until his knees buckled and he collapsed. Chad finally released his grip on the chain and hobbled away.

Josh kicked Wyatt in the face when he reached for Chad's ankle. "Stay down."

Reagan retrieved the brand from the fire and knelt over Wyatt. "You're finished." She took the hot iron and stabbed it into the side of his face. "Just look at you now. Disgusting hillbilly."

"Enough." Nick grabbed her arm, and Reagan shot him a sneer but released her hold on the brand. "Chad, are you okay?"

"I've been better." Chad forced himself to look away from Wyatt. "You guys saved me."

"We came here together, and we're leaving together." Josh, much to Chad's surprise, gave him an awkward pat on the back. "As long as we stick by each other, we can make it out of this."

For a moment, Chad almost believed him. It felt good to be a part of something real. Theirs was a bond forged in blood.

Then he saw the torchlight from outside the barn. "The cultists are coming. We have to go."

"This way," Josh said. "We found a trail we think leads to the abandoned town."

The group spilled into the woods and left Wyatt's crumpled form behind.

Wyatt woke to the sound of voices. It was dark inside the barn. The full moon had partially retreated behind the clouds, and the fire that burned inside the barrel had died away to nothing. He didn't know how much time had elapsed since the campers left him lying in his own filth. The voices couldn't belong to the kids, who were probably long gone by now.

No one had ever escaped from him before. Rage burned within him at the idea that a bunch of teenagers had managed to get the better of him. It was his game, and it wasn't over until he said it was.

I'll kill them. I'll strip the flesh from their bones.

Wyatt tried to prop himself up but collapsed under his own weight. His injuries were too many to count.

He heard the voices again. This time he stopped and listened. He wasn't alone. The voices were coming from outside the barn.

"They were here," someone said. "Spread out and search the area."

Wyatt crawled across the floor into the shadows to conceal himself. Torches glowed in the night, and he could make out the distinct outlines of hooded figures prowling the woods. Wyatt waited until the voices faded and all was quiet.

"You failed," a voice said from the dark.

Wyatt scanned the area for the voice's source, but the barn appeared empty. "Who's there? Show yourself."

The voice echoed through the barn so softly it was almost a hiss. "You allowed a group of children to overcome you. Pathetic. What would your father or brother think if they could see you now?"

"You don't know me."

As if born from the darkness itself, a figure appeared across from him. The blood moon re-emerged from the clouds to cast its light over a man in red robes. He held a scythe clutched in his hands, but it was his face that drew Wyatt's attention. An elk skull masked the man's head, and its horns seemed to merge with the shadows.

The figure knelt at Wyatt's side and whispered into his ear. "I know everything about you, Wyatt Carrow. I know what you discovered in the cave. I know what the voice said you could become if you consumed the flesh of the unworthy. We serve the same master."

"I serve myself." They were so close they might have touched, and yet Wyatt couldn't help feeling he was the only person inside the barn.

The eyes under the skull glowed with red light. "Even if unwittingly sacrificed, every life you have taken has been in service to a greater power. You have shed enough innocent blood to wake my master from his slumber. Baal rewards his followers, Wyatt."

"The voice in the cave is gone." Wyatt peered into the red eyes. "I haven't heard it in years."

"We can bring him back."

"How?"

"Finish what you have started. The campers must be sacrificed. When the earth is stained with their blood, the ritual will be complete. Now get up."

Strange words echoed across the wind like whispers, and Wyatt found himself filled with a renewed strength. He rose to tower over the figure in the elk mask. "Tell me more."

"One of their number bears a cross necklace. He blocks my path to the rest and must be removed. Do you understand?"

"Yes." Wyatt touched the scorched flesh on his face. "And Reagan?"

"Do what you want with her. She is no concern of mine."

Suddenly, Wyatt was alone inside the barn. He peered into the shadows, but the figure was gone, as if he had never been there at all.

It didn't matter. He knew what he needed to do. Wyatt loaded his rifle and slung the gun over his shoulder.

He always finished what he started.

Chapter SEVENTEEN

2:42 A.M.

The moon lit their path. The mountain's shadow crept over the valley as the group made their descent. Josh searched for the crows that had followed them, but the sky remained clear. Even so, he couldn't escape the feeling of being watched.

His legs ached from the journey. There was no telling how many miles they had trekked through the hills, and the others were clearly just as tired. Josh thought again of all they had suffered already. The cultists had drugged Brooke and attempted to sacrifice her on an altar. Reagan had been trapped in a madman's lair. Wyatt had shot Nick and beat Chad to within an inch of his life. Even Josh had been stabbed, though fortunately the wound was only a shallow one.

He took a mental inventory of their supplies. Only two flashlights remained between them. Reagan had lost her cell phone, and Brooke's had died. Nick's axe, cast aside by Wyatt, lay somewhere in the creek they'd left behind. Josh still had possession of the flare gun, but it had only one shot, and he had to make it count.

Despite everything, they had so far managed to survive a demonic cult, a murderous psychopath, a flock of relentless crows, and a possessed scarecrow. Maybe there was a chance for them to make it out alive. The abandoned settlement slid into view, and for the first time that night, Josh felt a surge of hope. With any luck, the road was nearby.

"We're here." Josh's flashlight illuminated a wooden sign at the town's border.

Torrent Falls, read the letters. *Population 186.*

"Finally." Reagan came to a stop. "I don't think I can go much farther."

"Be careful, everyone. Don't forget what happened at the mine." Josh took the lead, and the group quietly advanced into town.

From the look of things, the place had been uninhabited for a long time. The town, if it could really be called such, was more of an outpost. The few buildings were clustered together on either side of a dirt road that ran the length of the settlement. Josh guessed most of the town's former inhabitants had been associated with the mine in one way or another. When it dried up, so did the town.

At least we're out of the woods. That was a start.

His beam swept across the railroad's remains, rusted and decayed. Josh pictured the miners working long hours in insufferable conditions while the rich overseers prospered. He doubted they had access to electricity or running water. Hoping for reception, he took out his cell phone and waved it around, but there were still no bars.

"Look." Nick pointed his flashlight past the buildings. There, near the end of town and veiled in fog, loomed the road.

Josh felt a surge of relief and took off in a dead sprint for the road with the others in pursuit. An invisible wall barred him from setting foot beyond the town's border. He tried stepping forward again with the same result. It was as if the mist and the shadows had formed some kind of barrier that prevented his escape.

"It can't be." Josh paced along the barrier's length to find a break or a gap that might allow passage to the other side. There had to be some way to escape. He hadn't come this far for nothing. Surely there was something they could do. Josh stuck the barrier with his fists in anger before sinking to his knees in defeat. "We were so close." It was no use. He let the flare gun clatter to the ground.

Brooke tried stepping into the fog and also met resistance. "I don't understand. What's going on?"

Nick held out a hand and helped Josh to his feet. "I told you—we're trapped here."

Chad took the flare gun Josh had dropped and waved it in the air. "Someone will see it."

"Don't." Nick grabbed Chad's arm before he could pull the trigger. "Even if there was someone out there at this hour, what if the spell won't allow anyone outside the barrier to see us?"

Chad reluctantly eased his finger off the trigger and returned the flare gun to Josh. "I hope someone has an idea because it looks to me like we're out of options here."

"Bartholomew said his spell would keep us trapped here until dawn," Nick explained. "That must be how long the cultists have to complete the ritual. We're going to have to last the rest of the night if we want to survive."

"Then it's over." Reagan threw her hands up in despair. "There's nowhere else to go, and in case you've forgotten, we have a cult of devil worshipers and a living scarecrow after us."

Even Josh felt his confidence waning. "Sunrise isn't for another four hours."

"I know no one wants to hear this right now, but we're probably going to have to fight our way out of this." Nick looked at each of the others in turn. "We have to be ready when they come for us again. You've all seen the scarecrow's burns and how it hides from the light. It might be supernatural, but it's still made of straw."

"Nick's right." Josh cleared his throat. "We need to figure out our next move. I say we hunker down and hide out for now."

He retraced his steps to the largest building in town, an abandoned saloon with boarded-up windows. Josh pushed through batwing doors and entered a wide room full of cobwebs. A thick layer of dust clung to the room's decrepit furniture, and broken bottles were scattered across mostly empty shelves behind the bar.

"How's everyone holding up?" Josh took a seat at a table to rest his legs.

Chad massaged his broken nose. "I'm still in one piece, more or less."

"Thanks for coming back for me." Brooke aimed a smile at Chad. "It was very brave."

Chad started to laugh, but his bruised ribs promptly caused him to grimace. "Nobody's ever called me that before."

Nick spoke up. "Josh, I think you need to tell us more about what you learned online about the scarecrows."

Josh shrugged. "A lot of the information linked back to Gray Hollow's local newspaper. A journalist named Thomas Brooks wrote most of the stories. He was looking into some murders with the town sheriff, Jezebel Woods. According to what I found on Reddit, loads of creepy stuff has happened over the years in Gray Hollow."

"What kind of stuff?" Brooke, intrigued, leaned closer.

"For starters, people have been going missing there for a long time. Twenty years ago, a kid named Salem Alistair vanished."

"So?" Reagan crossed her arms.

"Salem Alistair built the scarecrows. All of them. The information online suggested the murders Thomas Brooks and Jezebel Woods were looking into were somehow connected to Salem's disappearance."

Reagan raised an eyebrow. "Connected?"

"As in, scarecrows kept popping up at the murder scenes."

"Anything else?" Nick asked.

"There were rumors that a settler started a group of demon worshipers in the 1700s, but nothing concrete. I found a lot of folklore and urban legends about the caves."

That sparked Brooke's interest. "When I was hiding from Wyatt inside the mine, I stumbled across one of the cave's entrances. Native Americans left symbols over the entrance warning about something evil inside the mountain. When I peeked into the entrance, I saw fire deep below. I can't explain it, but I felt a presence." She stopped, as if recalling something on the tip of her tongue. "Maybe it was the Keeper of the Crows."

Nick frowned. "Whatever is in there, Bartholomew wants to wake it up."

"I think he wants to finish what was started in Gray Hollow," Josh said.

"We can't let that happen."

Chad groaned. "We're just high schoolers. What can we do against something like that?"

No one answered.

Bartholomew ran his hand over the black book's cover. Whispers filled the air as he opened its pages. Containing the offerings inside a barrier of living darkness wasn't enough. Even the scarecrow had failed to kill the sacrifices thus far, though its strength was growing.

He hadn't believed they would last this long. It seemed almost impossible. Who were mere teenagers to defy him? Yet, somehow, they had survived everything set against them. Instead of falling apart, they had pulled together as one. It was time to invoke a more powerful spell.

The cultists heeded his call. He saw them approaching through his possession of the crows. The robed figures emerged from the cornstalks to form a circle around the altar. One of their number lowered her hood in a sign of contrition.

"I warned you not to disappoint me again, Rebecca."

She threw herself at his feet and begged for mercy. The air was thick with the stench of her fear. Bartholomew was thankful he was no longer human. The cultists had their uses, to be sure. He had used them for centuries, since he first offered the settlers power and secret knowledge in return for their absolute devotion. There were many facets of his master beyond the domain of Gray Hollow, and the cult continued his efforts in his absence.

It was through one of these servants, Percy Durer, that Baal had used Salem Alistair to raise an army of scarecrows and bring Gray Hollow to its knees. Jezebel Woods had destroyed the portion of Baal's spirit in Gray Hollow and nearly ruined all of his work. In the end, his followers were only human, and they would always fail, leaving Bartholomew—the last true prophet of Baal—to complete his master's work. He was so close now to reconstituting his master's physical form, and he would not allow his followers' incompetence to threaten everything he had labored for.

"Forgive me. I am your humble servant."

"You may still be of service, Rebecca."

She clutched the hem of his robes. "Anything."

He seized her by the hair and threw her on the altar.

"Help me." She looked to the others, but no one moved. They simply watched from the darkness under their hoods.

"Yes." His voice became a low hiss. "Give me your fear."

He uttered words from the book in a black tongue and swung the scythe through the air. Blood sprayed over the altar, and Rebecca fell still.

Crows swarmed from above down toward the corpse, engulfed the altar, and feasted on her remains. The earth shook as Bartholomew finished a spell that would give life to the campers' greatest fears.

One by one, they would surrender to their fear. It would consume and devour them until they were all dead.

The crows took to the sky and flocked toward the remains of Torrent Falls.

Chapter EIGHTEEN

3:32 A.M.

Nick was lost before he met Grace.

He left for college to escape an abusive home. It was a chance to start over and put his demons behind him. After spending his childhood standing up to his father to protect Josh and their mother, Nick wanted a normal life for a change. Although he had felt guilty about abandoning Josh, he told himself things at home would improve in his absence.

That was before his father murdered their mother, and Josh was forced to shoot him to defend himself. The news sent Nick spiraling into depression and despair. He wasn't there when Josh needed him the most. Even alcohol couldn't help him forget the pain. He failed out of college and struggled to make ends meet. For the first time in his life, he was truly alone.

Grace rescued him from himself. She changed his life forever. After driving her to the hospital, he'd bumped into her a few times on campus, and they struck up a friendship. She'd even invited him to church. Although it wasn't his particular cup of tea, he enjoyed being with her.

He didn't think their friendship would blossom into something more. Grace was different than the girls he'd dated before. She was funny, kind, and thoughtful. Their conversations were more meaningful. At the moment Nick thought he had lost everything, Grace helped him pick up the pieces.

The first time he had told her that he loved her, she didn't respond.

"Don't you feel the same way?" After all the effort it had taken him to say the words, after all he had seen his parents go through, Nick hadn't known how to handle it.

"Nick . . ." She trailed off, and it took her a long time to answer. "You know I'm going to die, right? Maybe not today, maybe not tomorrow—but it's going to happen."

Her illness had gone unspoken between them, but its presence was never far away.

"Why would a loving God allow you to suffer like this?"

"I honestly don't know. I don't understand His plan any more than you do. Maybe He wanted me to inspire others. Maybe He knew it was how I would meet you."

As Nick peered into the Appalachian wilderness outside the saloon, he tried to remember Grace's voice. He'd already begun to forget what it sounded like. Snoring broke his train of thought, and he looked back at the room's other occupant. "Chad?"

No answer. Chad, sound asleep, slumped over the table.

Nick stifled a yawn. The hour was late, and Chad wasn't the only person who was exhausted. They were supposed to be on the lookout while the others went to look for water, but as Nick watched Chad sleep, he decided against waking him.

Let the poor guy rest while he can. He'd been through enough. At least while he slept, Chad could escape the nightmare they were all trapped inside. In that respect, Nick envied him, but he couldn't rest. Not yet.

Floorboards rattled beneath his feet, and the walls of the saloon shook. Dust shaken loose by the commotion fell from the ceiling.

What's going on? Whatever it was, it probably wasn't anything good.

Nick left Chad behind and went outside for a better look. Crows flocked overhead as harsh words echoed through the sky, and the night was filled with hundreds of whispers. The earth trembled violently, and he grabbed a post to keep his footing.

Something's coming. I have to warn the others.

Nick switched on his flashlight and hurried toward the woods. He yelled for his brother and stared into the blackness beyond the trees. With the moon nearly hidden behind the clouds, it was difficult to see.

A voice called to him through the trees. "Nick."

"I'm here." He pushed through the brush and searched for the voice's source. "Josh?"

The mist parted to reveal a small child kneeling over a body. Nick stopped dead in his tracks. This wasn't right. His mind screamed at him to run, but he couldn't bring himself to look away.

The boy's sobs broke the sudden stillness.

"Are you okay?"

The boy turned around. It was Josh, but as a child. Blood covered his face and hands. The body on the ground was their father's.

"Why did you leave me, Nick?"

"You're not real." Nick stammered the words. "This isn't real." He took a step back, and the boy vanished as the mist closed in around him.

"Nick," a woman's voice said. "You left me to die."

A shadowy figure approached in the dark. Nick shined the light at her. His mother's face, rotted and decayed, looked back.

Josh and the others gathered beside the creek. Brooke knelt over the bank and gulped down a mouthful of cold water while Reagan filled a canteen to take back to Nick and Chad. Josh, keeping watch with the flashlight, remained on the lookout.

The expedition wasn't a complete failure. In addition to locating the creek, Josh had discovered a forest path at the town border that appeared to lead back to the mines. A steep cliff promised a precipitous drop into the mists below for anyone who ventured too close, but apart from a few more barns scattered in close proximity to Torrent Falls, there really wasn't much else to find.

The moonlight faded, and a voice reverberated through his head like thunder. Wincing, Josh dropped to his knees and pressed his hands against his head while the earth shifted under him. Finally, the voice faded. As the tremors subsided, the mist at the forest's edge crept forward and licked at his shoes.

"What's going on?" Brooke seemed to have been affected in a similar fashion. "What was that?"

Josh helped her to her feet. "I don't know." He glanced toward town, where crows swarmed across the sky. "We should get back."

Brooke lingered behind when he started forward. "Where's Reagan?"

Josh swept the area with the flashlight, but Reagan was nowhere in sight.

"Reagan!" His voice echoed through the darkness.

For a moment, he heard nothing. Then the night was filled with the sound of crows. The flock diverted from Torrent Falls and swarmed the forest.

Josh pushed Brooke forward one second before the crows engulfed him. The birds pecked and tore at him with their claws until Josh tore free of the swarm and fought his way through the fog. "Brooke?"

She, too, was gone. He was alone—or was he? Whispers called to him from within the mist.

"Who's there?" Josh started forward with the flashlight, and the mist parted to uncover a tombstone. *What's that doing here?*

A lone grave in the middle of the woods didn't make any sense at all. His beam illuminated the name etched into the stone, and Josh's mouth fell open in horror.

Thomas Rush, read the name on the stone.

Josh stared in shock at his father's grave. *It can't be.*

The ground opened up beneath his feet, and a hand latched onto his ankle. Josh fell back, and the flashlight rolled from his grasp. The beam, which came to rest a short distance away, illuminated a massive form rising from the earth.

"Son." His father loomed before him. A gaping hole occupied the place where his heart should have been.

"You're dead. I killed you."

Dark laughter emanated from his father's corpse, which somehow spoke despite a rotted lower jaw. "You can't kill me, Josh. I'm a part of you."

His father staggered toward him with arms outstretched for a final embrace.

Chad woke to the sound of whispers. *I must have fallen asleep.*

"Nick?" He rubbed the sleep from his eyes.

No one answered. He glanced around the saloon, but the room was abandoned. Chad nearly fell out of the chair scrambling to his feet.

"Guys?"

The night was eerily quiet. Where had everyone gone?

Maybe they left you behind, said a voice in the back of his mind.

He heard something coming from outside the building. The floor-boards sagged under his weight. It sounded like whispers—hundreds of whispers. He couldn't make out what they were saying, but they seemed to be calling to him. Chad walked outside the saloon, where a mist had fallen over the ghost town.

Chad searched for the whispers' source, but it was difficult to see in the darkness. *What happened to the moon?*

He squinted in the minimal light. The abandoned settlement was even more unsettling without the others around. When he looked at the buildings lining the road, he saw shadowy figures watching from the windows, like wraiths waiting to claim him.

He quickened his pace and concentrated on the whispers. They were getting closer. What were they saying?

"Chad," one of the voices called, and he discerned the faint impressions of outlines in the gathering fog.

"Josh?" He felt a surge of relief. "Thank God. Where did you go?"

"We left you, Chad," Brooke's voice said. "You were dragging us down."

"You're such a disappointment," Reagan said, but it was his father's voice he heard.

Chad stopped just short of the figures concealed in the mist. Something was wrong. The voices were distorted—not quite right. "Guys?"

The receding mist unveiled the others. Living shadows wrapped around their skin. Their eyes burned like fire in the night, and their hands were shaped like claws.

"The crows are hungry, Chad," Josh said. "The Keeper needs blood."

Reagan held her hand out to him. "Come to us, Chad. It'll be over fast. Then we can be together again—forever."

Horrified, Chad took a step back, and Reagan's expression turned to one of monstrous rage. He fled into the woods as fast as he could go.

"Running again," one of the voices said. "You'll always be a coward, Chad."

"Why are you doing this?" Even in the dark, he felt them behind him.

"Did you really think we were your friends? No one cares about you. You don't matter to anyone."

"Leave me alone!"

"But you are alone," a voice echoed, though now it was so distorted he could no longer tell to whom it belonged.

The whispers faded. When he looked back, the figures were gone. Torrent Falls was only faintly visible past the trees. Something moved in the brush nearby, and the scarecrow stepped into the moonlight.

Reagan didn't care where the others had gone. She just wanted to make the voices stop. The whispers were everywhere, but no matter where she looked, she couldn't see where they were coming from.

What's happening to me? She saw flashes of crows whenever she tried closing her eyes.

You know what's happening, a voice said inside her head. *You've always known.*

"This isn't happening." She covered her ears to block out the whispers. "This isn't real."

Of course, the voice replied. *That's the point.*

"Get out of my head." She tried and failed to keep from trembling.

You're losing it, Reagan—just like you always feared.

Reagan screamed at the top of her lungs. "Shut up, shut up, shut up!" She ran through the woods with reckless abandon while manic laughter followed.

She stumbled through the creek and caught a glimpse of her reflection. Reagan didn't recognize the face looking back at her. It was the wrinkled face of an old woman with gray hair and lifeless eyes. She put her hands up to her face in horror. It was her mother's face—the face of madness.

"No!" She fell to her knees and sobbed into her hands.

"I can make the voices stop," a voice said. "Forever."

When Reagan opened her eyes again, she was staring once more at her youthful, beautiful face. A figure approached through the mist. The horns of the elk skull he wore seemed to move.

"You." She stiffened instinctively. "What do you want from me?"

"I want to make you whole again, Reagan. Wouldn't you like that?"

"How do you know my name?" She should have been terrified, but there was something about him she couldn't run from, even if she wanted to.

"I know everything about you, Reagan, even the parts you try to hide from yourself. The fear of losing your mind, for instance—I can take that from you."

"Why would you help me?" She was unable to look away from the dark spaces where his eyes should have been.

As he spoke, they glowed with red light. "You're not like the others, Reagan. I could use someone like you at my side. Serve the Keeper of the Crows, and you can live forever, young and beautiful."

"I don't believe in angels and demons. They're just made-up fairytales. They don't exist."

"But they believe in you. Consider my words. You need not die here with your friends."

She looked once more at her reflection in the water and shivered at the thought of the crone that had stared back at her. "What do I have to do in return?"

Shadows coalesced in his hands, forming a blade, and suddenly he was clutching a knife. "Kill them. They will be your sacrifice."

Reagan hesitated when he held it out to her.

"Take it." His voice was firmer.

Her hands shaking, Reagan grabbed the knife. It felt surprisingly cool to the touch.

Then, he was gone.

You should do it, the voice said as she turned the blade over in her hands. *It might even be fun.*

Chapter NINETEEN

3:49 A.M.

Nick's world threatened to spin out of control. Everywhere he turned, another horrific scene from the past confronted him. Twisted facsimiles of Josh and their parents brought up all the ways he'd failed them while converging on him.

"Why did you leave us, Nick?" His mother's corpse decayed further with each passing second.

"You promised you would take me with you," the boy version of Josh reminded him. "You said you would protect me."

His father wore a twisted smile. "You're just like me, son."

The mist rose as they circled him, and the whispers filled his mind with images of Josh and his mother suffering at the hands of his father. Powerless, Nick could only watch. He struggled not to resign himself to despair, but his knees buckled under the weight of his guilt.

Another voice came from the night. "Don't give in. This isn't real."

In the midst of near-total darkness, a speck of light glowed. Nick forgot his fear and reached toward the light, which grew in intensity until it was so bright that he could hardly look at it. Nick, shielding his eyes, found himself pulled into another memory.

When the white glare subsided, he was looking at his feet on a white tile floor. The forest and the mist were gone, replaced by a quiet hospital room. He sat in a chair, holding Grace's hand. She wore a hospital gown.

"I won't know what to do without you." Nick's eyes burned with tears. "I'll be lost."

Grace squeezed his hand. Even tired and sick, she had a surprising strength. "God still has a plan for you, Nick. Maybe you can start by reaching out to your brother."

"I wouldn't even know where to begin."

She pointed to his chest. "Trust your heart, and you'll find a way to make it right."

The memory changed, and doctors and nurses surrounded the bed while alarms rang from the monitors. Grace's mother sobbed in her husband's arms. Nick, unable to move, pressed up against the wall and watched. He was too stunned to even cry.

Hooked up to the ventilator, Grace was unable to speak. Her hand opened, and the cross necklace fell to the ground.

"Wake up," her voice said.

Suddenly, Nick found himself in the forest once more. The spectral images of his family were gone. With the memory gone, he was able to recognize that they were just visions, likely created by one of Bartholomew's spells.

Something gleamed ahead in the fog. *Wyatt.* A rifle's barrel glimmered in the re-emerged moon's light.

Nick dropped to the ground. Seconds later, a gunshot resounded.

He expects me to run. If he did, Wyatt would have little trouble picking him off. Instead, Nick charged forward and rammed into Wyatt. If Wyatt had braced himself, his size would have protected him, but he was taken by surprise, and the collision sent them both sprawling to the ground.

Wyatt pounced on him, and his massive hands wrapped around Nick's neck. As the air drained from his lungs, Nick grasped at the earth until his hand closed around a rock. He brought it up hard against Wyatt's head and kicked his way free. Hobbling for the trees, Nick looked back to see Wyatt fumbling for his rifle.

I have to find Josh and the others before it's too late.

Chad's entire body hurt from the effort, but he had to keep moving. He ran as fast as his injured ankle permitted while looking for a place to hide. Surely the mine and the town weren't the only spots he could seek refuge. There had to be another cabin, or a barn like the one Wyatt had held him captive in.

He found himself unable to resist the urge to look over his shoulder, where the scarecrow's silhouette remained visible in the darkness. Chad finally understood that the vision of his pursuers had been a ruse meant to lure him away from town, and he had fallen for it. He had run right into the scarecrow, and now the others would never know where he'd gone.

He finally collapsed underneath a towering oak tree. His breathing faded to a low whimper, and he tried his best to stay still. The night grew quiet, and he poked his head out from behind the tree to see if the scarecrow had lost his trail. Then he heard it shuffling along the forest floor, and his eyes fell on the spot where it was searching for him. Chad moved from tree to tree and kept out of sight as it advanced through the woods. He began to stand up to move to the next tree when the pitchfork plunged into the tree. Chad tried to move and found his letterman jacket pinned to the tree by the pitchfork.

Moonlight seeped through the treetops as the scarecrow emerged from the fog. With growing desperation, Chad struggled to free himself while the scarecrow grew nearer. At the last moment, he slid free of the letterman jacket and landed on the ground. The scarecrow plucked the pitchfork from the tree and raised it over him, but he pulled his legs back an instant before it drove the weapon into the earth.

His victory was short-lived, as the scarecrow grabbed him from behind and tossed him through the air into a tree. The impact rattled his teeth, and before he could find his footing, the scarecrow seized him, lifted him into the air, and pinned him against the tree.

As its fingers inched toward his eyes, Chad reached down and thrust his hand into the hole in its chest where Josh had plunged the knife. The scarecrow's insides, a mixture of straw and ash, sent a chill flooding through his veins. The scarecrow's burlap face contorted, seemingly in anger, and it flung him across the clearing. He hit the ground hard beside the pitchfork.

Chad grabbed the pitchfork's handle and struggled to liberate it from the earth as the scarecrow drew closer. The pitchfork slid free at the last second, and Chad swung it with all the strength he had. The scarecrow let out a shriek as the spikes impaled its throat and severed some of the threads between its head and its body. Its head fell partially to one side, and it grabbed the pitchfork's handle and flung Chad toward the bushes. He took advantage of the distance between them to flee up a steep path leading farther along the mountain.

An old rope bridge materialized ahead. As he burst past the trees, the scarecrow raised its arms, and a swarm of crows covered the sky. Chad tried to run at full speed, but his ankle slowed him down. A quick glance over the rickety bridge's side told him the drop down, ending in rocks, was unmistakably fatal. Many of the wooden steps were rotten or altogether missing. Chad looked back and saw the scarecrow following close behind. There wasn't another option.

When he was just over halfway across, his leg burst through one of the steps, and he nearly fell. Chad clawed his way upright as the crows descended on the bridge to peck and tear at the fraying ropes. Swatting the birds away, he abandoned all pretense of caution and broke into a sprint. As the bridge collapsed, Chad threw himself forward. He reached out and clutched the torn ropes affixed to the wooden beams on the other side, wincing as his body and the remaining planks slammed into the side of the cliff. He dangled there and watched the rest of the bridge vanish into the dark abyss. Using the broken section of bridge as a ladder, he pulled himself over the ledge to safety.

The scarecrow watched him from the other side. Chad followed its gaze farther up the mountain, where torchlight appeared. The cult was coming. When he looked back at the scarecrow, its stitched smile seemed to grow. He heard screams coming from the valley, and the scarecrow retreated into the forest in search of new prey.

Chad wanted nothing more than to lie there and catch his breath, but the torches were growing closer with every second. He climbed to his feet and stumbled through the woods while dragging his injured leg behind him. He glanced back to make sure he hadn't been followed. With sparse moonlight to guide his path, he didn't see the rock wall until it was too late. His head collided with it, and everything went black.

Josh was lost, and he couldn't find his way back. He fled from his father, who grew increasingly monstrous looking the farther Josh went.

His father's menacing voice called from the trees. "Come on out, son. You've been misbehaving again. It's time for your punishment."

Don't listen to him.

His father stepped out of the shadows. "Look at you, sniveling like a coward." His father's voice dripped with contempt. Blood trickled from the hole in his chest. "That's why you couldn't save your mother."

Josh's anger overcame his fear. He threw himself on top of his father and hit him again and again as the whispers cheered him on in the background. When Josh finally lowered his bloodstained hands, it wasn't his father's face staring back at him, but his own. Josh peered into his own eyes, reflecting all his self-loathing magnified into something monstrous.

"This is what you are," his double said. "It is all you'll ever be—ugly, broken, and alone."

Someone else called out to him. "Don't listen to them, Josh."

"What?" His brow furrowed in confusion. *Was that Nick's voice?*

"Don't listen to the whispers." Nick put a hand on his back. "It isn't real."

"He's lying," the other Josh said. "You killed them."

"I killed them," Josh repeated, as if in a trance.

Nick looked at him with compassion. "You have to let it go. You have to forgive yourself."

"Murderer," the other Josh growled.

Josh, confronted with his own reflection, finally shook his head. *It wasn't my fault.*

He blinked, and the blood was gone from his hands. He knelt on the ground with Nick beside him. There were no gravestones, no bodies anywhere in sight—his father's or otherwise. "Nick?"

"It's all right. I'm here." Nick wrapped him in a tight embrace.

Josh let himself cry for the first time since the night his parents died. "She's dead, Nick. They're both dead."

"I know. I'm sorry—for everything."

Josh sobbed into his brother's shoulder, and they stayed like that for several minutes until Josh wiped his tears away.

"Where's Chad?"

Nick helped him to his feet. "He was asleep when I left the saloon. What about the others?"

Josh shrugged. "I forgot all about them when I lost it."

"You weren't the only one seeing things. I saw some pretty messed-up stuff, too."

Josh thought again of the whispers. "Bartholomew must have cast another spell. If you hadn't snapped me out of it when you did . . ."

"That's not all. Wyatt's still out there. He knows we're here, and the scarecrow probably isn't far away."

Josh tensed as a scream echoed through the woods. "Brooke." He hurried toward the sound and hoped he wasn't too late.

They found her curled up in a ball. Although her eyes were open, she didn't appear to notice their approach. Instead, she was staring past them at something only she could see.

"Please, don't hurt Josh. I'll do whatever you want."

The hair on Josh's arms stood up as he realized she was talking about *him*. Losing *him* was her biggest fear? All that time when he thought he was alone—that nothing really meant anything—he'd been wrong.

"It's all right." He took her by the hand. "I'm here."

She acknowledged him at last. "Josh?"

He hugged her. "Yeah, Brooke. It's me."

She looked at him as if he were a ghost. "I thought you were dead."

"It was an illusion," Nick said. "One of Bartholomew's tricks."

Josh let go of Brooke. "Where's Reagan?" She'd vanished around the time the visions started.

"I don't know. I can't remember. It seemed so real."

Josh nodded. "How did you manage to break free, Nick?"

"I had some help." While not elaborating, Nick unconsciously fingered the cross necklace. "Chad and Reagan were probably affected too. We need to find them before anyone else does."

Nick stopped short. Josh followed his gaze and saw the mountain covered in firelight. The cult was descending on Torrent Falls.

"We have to make it back to town. The others could still be there."

They took off in the town's direction while thunder crashed across the endless black expanse. The faint outline of buildings grew clearer at their approach. The sliver of moonlight that escaped the clouds shrouded Torrent Falls in an ethereal glow. Crows flocked overhead in the hundreds, and their wings cast moving shadows over the earth.

When they reached the settlement, a shadowy figure emerged from the dark, and Josh's eyes fell on the scarecrow by the town sign.

Brooke slipped and fell to the ground behind them. Josh sprinted back and helped her to her feet, and they stumbled toward the saloon together as the scarecrow advanced.

Nick peered inside. "Chad's gone, and I don't see Reagan, either."

Josh glanced over his shoulder. The scarecrow drew closer, and hooded figures had appeared on the town's edge. Without warning, a gunshot reverberated through the night, and a bullet hit the saloon. Josh saw Wyatt's silhouette towering in the distance.

Brooke watched as their enemies closed in around them. "What are we going to do?"

"I'll hold them off," Nick volunteered.

Josh shook his head. "No way. We're not leaving you."

"Listen to me for a second." Nick put his hands on Josh's shoulders. "You're going to make it out of this. Find Thomas Brooks. Tell him what Bartholomew has planned for Gray Hollow." The approaching cultists headed straight for them. "Now go!" Nick shoved him forward.

Josh took Brooke's hand, and as they fled across the open field, he remembered the forest path he'd discovered that led back to the mines. His gaze fell on a barn outside of town near where they'd found the path.

Two cultists emerged from the trees and swung their torches at them. Josh punched one in the face, and Brooke bit the other's arm as he tried to restrain her. They outpaced their pursuers and sprinted toward the barn with the crows following overhead. Below, the ledge running along the barrier dropped off into the darkness.

The barn was quiet. Josh struggled to shut the massive wooden door to prevent the cultists from following them inside as Brooke started toward the back entrance. Without warning, a force collided with the other side of the door and knocked him off his feet. The scarecrow loomed over him in the pale moonlight. Josh fumbled with the flare gun in his pocket, but the scarecrow knocked it aside with its pitchfork.

"Josh!" Brooke started forward, but it was too late for her to reach him in time.

The scarecrow raised the pitchfork to strike him.

Nick spotted the scarecrow headed in his brother's direction and followed it to the barn. Nick tackled the scarecrow and sent them both rolling across the ground. The rest of the cultists were on their way, and Wyatt was still out there, but right now, saving Josh was the only thing that mattered.

Josh, stunned, regarded him from across the barn floor. Brooke, at the barn's back entrance, clasped a hand over her mouth. As the scarecrow climbed to its feet, Nick gestured for the others to stay back.

"Get out of here." He picked himself up.

When the scarecrow reached again for Josh, Nick threw himself at it with everything he had. Each blow glanced off its surface and barely impacted it at all. The scarecrow slammed him against the wall as Brooke helped Josh to his feet. It started toward them, but Nick charged at it again.

"Go!" He struggled with the scarecrow for possession of the pitchfork as Josh and Brooke fled the barn.

The scarecrow pushed with all its might, but Nick didn't budge. He'd made it this far, and he wasn't about to lose his chance to save his brother—to save everyone. The scarecrow's face twisted into something resembling surprise as Nick pushed it back, directly under the hayloft. Before it could react, he pulled the rope, opening the hatch. Hay flooded over the scarecrow and buried it underneath.

Nick let out a relieved sigh and rummaged through the hay for the flare gun Josh had dropped. *It has to be around here somewhere.*

The scarecrow's hand shot out from beneath the pile, and he quickened his pace. His hand closed around the handle at the same time the scarecrow clawed its way to the surface.

Nick pointed the flare gun triumphantly at the scarecrow. He pictured the flames consuming it and ending the cult's sick game once and for all.

Before he could pull the trigger, a blast echoed outside the barn, and a bullet ripped into his shoulder. His aim went wild. The flare struck the floor and sent a wall of flame spreading across the barn between him and the scarecrow.

Nick dropped the flare gun and stumbled out of the barn, after his brother. At least Josh was safe. Josh and Brooke looked back at him from the path ahead. Nick made eye contact with his brother from across the field and smiled to show Josh he was all right. As Nick started toward them, Josh's mouth dropped open in horror. Hundreds of shrieks filled the air, and Nick glanced up in time to see the entire mass of crows flocking toward him.

It was too late to run. Nick reached out to his brother just before the swarm struck him head-on and carried him over the ledge and into the darkness below.

Chapter TWENTY

Josh had made a mistake. The path he'd discovered didn't lead to the mine. He wasn't sure *where* it led, but one thing was certain—they couldn't go back. He hoped Chad and Reagan were still out there somewhere, but as far as he knew, only he and Brooke were left.

Brooke's hand tightened around his. Was it out of fear, or did she want to comfort him? Josh came to a stop and stared down the mountain. The hike had taken a lot out of him. Although he was accustomed to staying up till all hours of the night, this was a different kind of exhaustion. He wasn't sure how much farther he could go without rest.

Torrent Falls was no longer visible. Neither were the torches below. The moonlight that peeked through bare branches grew fainter as the forest spread around them. Fortunately, Josh still had his flashlight— their last defense against the dark—and his pocketknife.

Brooke was the first to give voice to his unspoken concern. "Where are we?"

"I'm not sure. Nothing looks familiar."

He wasn't surprised. The forest was enormous. They had barely scratched the surface in the daylight hours. They were lucky to have found their way so far. Josh suspected they were somewhere between the mines and the farm, though how close to either he couldn't tell.

"The air feels colder in this part of the forest." Brooke shuddered. "How are you holding up?"

Josh kept his feelings bottled up. Nick's death was still raw. The haziness of adrenaline, injury, and fatigue was almost a blessing, protecting him from fully processing his brother's demise. They needed to keep going, and he had to be strong—for both their sakes.

When a twig snapped nearby, he switched off the flashlight. "Stay low." They hid under the bushes. A few moments later, a figure advanced through the shadows, and Josh braced himself to attack if necessary.

"Hello? Is someone there?" Reagan stepped into the moonlight.

"It's us." Josh hurried to meet her. "I'm glad you made it out. We were worried."

Brooke stared past her. "Where's Chad?"

"I haven't seen anyone since I was separated from the group." Reagan flashed an odd smile. "I'm so glad I found you."

"How *did* you find us?" Brooke almost sounded suspicious. "Where have you been?"

"I thought I heard voices. What about Nick?"

Josh stared at his feet and finally forced himself to say the words aloud. "He's gone."

Brooke put her hand on his shoulder to reassure him, but Reagan greeted the news with a strange expression. It was almost as if she were relieved.

"Come with me." Reagan beckoned to them to follow her. "I think I found a way out of here."

Josh's brow furrowed. "How?"

"Keep your voice down. I'll explain when we get there." Reagan led them deeper into the forest until the moonlight vanished completely.

Josh kept his voice a whisper. "Are you sure you know where you're going?" How could she see so easily in the dark?

"This way."

They came to a stop outside the trees' border, where his flashlight's beam fell on a cave's opening.

Brooke went still. "I remember this place. What are we doing here?"

"I found something inside." Reagan stared into the cave's infinite darkness. "Something that can help us."

Brooke crossed her arms. "I have a bad feeling about this place. Tell us just what it is you think you found in the cave that you think could help us."

"Shh! Do you hear that?" Reagan looked around, and Josh followed her gaze. "Oh, never mind. If you're so worried, Brooke, you should stay here and keep watch." She yanked Josh toward the cave's entrance. "Come on, or we won't have time to get what we need before they come for us."

Josh glanced back at Brooke, who took a step after him, and then held up his hand to indicate that she should wait. She dutifully planted herself at the mouth of the cave, her face a mixture of disapproval and disbelief.

Once inside the cave, Josh moved his beam from one side to the next and frowned. Brooke was right. Something *did* feel off. Wasn't the cave the last place they should be?

"Shouldn't we be out there looking for Chad?"

"I needed to talk to you alone." Reagan stood on her tiptoes and reached for his face. "Forget Chad. We don't need him. We don't need anyone."

"What? What about Brooke?"

"What about her? She'll only slow us down." Reagan kissed him hard on the lips. "I love you, Josh."

Josh wanted to keep holding her in his arms. He had longed to hear those words for so long, but something was wrong.

"Leave her here. It'll just be the two of us, the way it was always supposed to be."

Josh stared at her for a long moment in the dim light within the cave, and for the first time, he looked past her beauty and saw the true measure of the cruelty underneath.

"Never." He felt a sense of shame mingled with disgust. He turned away and started for the cave entrance.

"I'm sorry to hear that. I really am."

He felt a sharp pain in his back and stumbled to his knees. When he looked up, Reagan stood over him holding a knife covered in blood—his blood. For a moment he thought he saw red light emanating from deeper within the cave.

"Reagan? What are you doing?"

"It has to be this way. Once you're all dead, the voices will finally stop." She started toward him, but Brooke emerged from the darkness and bashed her head with a rock. Reagan fell to the ground.

"She stabbed me." Josh reached for Brooke's outstretched hand. "Is she dead?"

Brooke prodded Reagan with her foot. "No. Just unconscious." She helped Josh to his feet and let him lean against her for support. "We can't stay here."

The cave trembled under their feet as they fled.

Chad groaned and sat up.

Where am I? He didn't remember anything after running across the bridge to escape the scarecrow. Hitting the rock wall must have given him a concussion. Ironically, his unintentional rest left him more recovered from the brutal beating Wyatt had inflicted on him earlier that night. He still felt terrible, but at least he could move without too much pain.

He peered out of the one eye that wasn't completely swollen shut and took in his surroundings. *I hope the others are okay.* With the bridge out, there was nothing he could do for them now. Still, there were other paths that led up the mountain. There was a chance they'd made it out, but at the moment he couldn't afford to worry about that.

Voices sounded ahead, and Chad crawled, keeping low. A pair of hooded figures rushed past him with torches burning brightly in the night.

What time is it? There was no telling how long he had been unconscious. Surely daylight couldn't be *that* far away. He just had to figure out how best to survive until then. Chad climbed to his feet and advanced through the forest with as much stealth as he could muster. With dawn on the horizon, the cultists were probably getting desperate.

He pushed through some bushes and came face-to-face with another cultist.

Chad swore under his breath, lowered his head, and tackled the cultist before the man could call out to his companions. The move caught the cultist by surprise, and they both went rolling downhill. Chad landed on top and rained down punches on the body beneath him until the figure slumped over.

I guess football practice wasn't a waste after all.

Chad started to climb to his feet when he spotted the scarecrow following the crows nearby. He couldn't escape the feeling it was looking for him.

They came upon an old church in the middle of the woods. The steeple cast a shadow over them in the moonlight. Peeling white paint exposed gray boards underneath. One of the black doors had rusted off its hinges and fallen inward.

"In here." Brooke helped him inside.

Josh didn't protest. He couldn't remember the last time he had rested.

Pale light filtering in through the dust-covered windows pierced the darkness inside the church. Their footsteps echoed across the wooden floor. Exhausted, Josh plopped down in front of the altar. Brooke settled beside him, and together they took advantage of the peace while it lasted.

"Do really you think the fog will lift if we make it until morning?" Brooke asked.

"Maybe." He tried to sound optimistic for her sake. It seemed just as likely that Bartholomew's spell would keep them trapped in an eternal night until the ritual was complete. "I can't believe Reagan tried to kill me."

Brooke traced the spot where Reagan had stabbed him. "Let me take a look at it."

Josh grimaced when she lifted his shirt. "How does it look?"

"Bad, but I don't think you're going to die from it. Not yet, at least."

"Thanks. I mean it, Brooke—and not just for tonight. You've always been there for me."

"You know how I feel about you. I . . . I love you, Josh."

Josh found himself taken aback by her naked vulnerability. He sought out her hand in the dark, and their faces drifted closer together until at last their lips met.

Brooke laughed. "It's funny that it took something like this for me to tell you how I feel."

Josh smiled at her. "There's a lot I would change about tonight, but not this."

Without warning, the remaining door came crashing down, and the scarecrow's monstrous form took shape in the entrance. Josh and Brooke leaped to their feet, but there was nowhere to go.

A hiss echoed from within the scarecrow's stitched mouth, and it shambled toward them while dragging the pitchfork behind it.

Josh brought the flashlight up and shined the beam directly into the scarecrow's eyes. When the scarecrow flinched instinctively from the light, Josh flung himself at it, knocking it aside as he and Brooke raced toward the exit. The scarecrow's hand shot out and grabbed Josh's ankle, but Brooke kicked it in the face, and Josh slipped out of its grasp.

Chad's voice rang out across the woods. "This way!" He waved his hands to get their attention, and he sprinted to meet them. "Man, am I glad to see you. I thought you were goners for sure."

"You too." Josh looked back and saw the shadowy figure rise at the church's entrance. "Where are we going?"

"The railroad tracks—I found them again, with help from one of the cultists, actually. I saw the scarecrow and followed you guys here."

When he saw the tracks, Josh realized where they were. *This path will take us back to the cabin.*

"Look out!" Brooke exclaimed seconds before the scarecrow hurled its pitchfork at them. It missed her by inches, and she slipped and hit the ground as the scarecrow approached.

Josh threw himself at the scarecrow. The impact sent them both over an embankment and plunging into the pond. Cold water rushed over him as he slipped under the surface. He emerged in the dark and looked around for the scarecrow, but the mist-covered pond only rippled serenely from his treading.

Suddenly, the scarecrow's burlap face pressed against his skin, and two hands dragged him back underwater. Josh struggled in vain to free himself. If he didn't do something soon, he would drown. Thinking quickly, he reached into his pocket, gripped his pocketknife, and in one fluid motion, he cut the button eye from the scarecrow's face. Its hold broke, and he burst to the surface and gasped for air.

Josh waded toward the bank, where Chad and Brooke pulled him onto the hard ground. He stared at the pocketknife, a gift from Nick when they were younger. After everything that had happened between them, he had thought about getting rid of it so many times but never could quite bring himself to do so. Now it had probably saved his life.

The scarecrow shrieked and thrashed about as if in pain. Unable to see them, it blindly swiped the air. The crows cawed in the distance, and the scarecrow turned and lumbered in their direction with slow and labored movements. Josh saw its burns in the moonlight. Nick's sacrifice hadn't been in vain.

It's weakened.

"Where is it headed?" Brooke asked.

The scarecrow didn't seem to be looking for them at all. Instead, it dragged itself along the railroad tracks like it was in a trance.

Chad clenched his teeth. "That's the same way the cultists were going."

Josh suddenly realized where it was headed. "The farm. They're all going back to the farm."

He wasn't sure what, but something big was definitely about to happen.

Everything would be over soon. It was time to bring the night to its intended conclusion. Dawn approached. Nothing could be left to chance, not when he was so close.

Bartholomew remained within the circle, as he had since the ritual began. It was the source of his connection to his master and his power over the land. Although he could project his consciousness elsewhere, the ritual would end if he physically left the circle.

The wind whispered softly and carried word from the crows discernable only to him. Somehow, his spell had failed. Or, rather, the one with the cross necklace had managed to resist his will and break his hold over the others. It was inconceivable that a mere adolescent could contest his power, but no matter. Nick Rush was dead. Through the crows, Bartholomew had watched him fall.

His followers gathered around him, and he beckoned for them to join him inside the circle. The only sound came from the crows flocking above. Bartholomew listened until he heard movement within the cornfield. Slowly, the scarecrow emerged from the stalks. He could feel the others' fear at the sight of its mangled form.

It dropped the pitchfork and shuffled over to him, and Bartholomew inspected it. The scarecrow had already been damaged when the cult recovered it. Now, the power used to animate it was barely enough to hold it together. Its head was almost detached, and a large hole had been cut into its chest. New burns covered its body.

"The time has come. Hear me, Keeper of the Crows. I offer you all of my remaining followers to give your child life."

Bartholomew raised the scythe high toward the blood moon. The crows descended toward him in a pillar of shadow, and their shrieks became a roar. The others tried to run, but it was too late. The swarm devoured the cultists, and their cries faded as the life was drained from them.

The scarecrow opened its mouth as the crows flocked toward it. It swallowed the darkness whole. Its injuries faded until only a small patch of burned burlap remained behind, and its claw-like hands curled into fists.

Bartholomew surveyed the corpses as the scarecrow retrieved its pitchfork and returned to the cornfield.

Chapter TWENTY-ONE

4:48 A.M.

From the moment she first laid eyes on it, Brooke had thought there was something sinister about the cabin. Now they found themselves again at the campsite. If she'd only tried harder to convince the others of what she had seen in the woods, maybe they wouldn't be in such a mess. So much had happened since then, and the night wasn't over yet.

Brooke inspected the campsite to make sure they were alone. There were no crows in sight that might give away their presence. Almost nothing had changed since their departure. The campsite appeared frozen in time, as if impervious to their ordeal. When her gaze fell on the bloody handprint on the cabin's open door, she wondered how many other unsuspecting victims had suffered the same fate and how many might follow in their footsteps. The Natives were right. The land *was* cursed.

"At least we know where we are." Chad, on the verge of exhaustion, struggled to keep up. "That has to count for something, right?"

He looked like he had been through hell. He was bloodied and bruised from Wyatt's beating. It was a miracle he was still standing, and yet he seemed to have found an inner strength that Brooke wouldn't have guessed he possessed. If there was one takeaway from their shared nightmare, it was that she'd learned they all had hidden depths. They'd all found something in themselves to keep going. It was the only way they could have survived so long.

Chad collapsed onto one of the logs surrounding the burned-out campfire, and Brooke sank onto the one beside him, while Josh attempted to start a fire using supplies from the kit. Brooke stared into the pot as the flames stirring to life ate away at the kindling. Only one night ago she sat in the same spot eating smores, telling stories, and feeling jealous of Reagan. That felt like a lifetime ago.

"We can't stay here." She looked at each of the others in turn. "They know to look for us here."

Chad groaned. "What about the others? There's a chance they could find their way back here. That's how we all met up the first time."

"That thing killed my brother." Josh's hands balled into fists. "I'm done hiding."

"Nick?" Chad appeared genuinely upset by the news. "I'm sorry. He was a good guy." He hesitated. "What about Reagan?"

Brooke interjected. "She went psycho and tried to kill Josh before I knocked her out. We left her in the cave."

"You're kidding me." Chad might have raised an eyebrow in surprise, but given his degree of facial swelling, it was difficult to tell. "Even for Reagan, that's pretty messed up."

Josh shook his head. "It wasn't her. At least I don't think it was. Somehow Bartholomew got inside her head."

"I saw some crazy stuff myself." Chad's expression grew distant.

Brooke held her hands up to the fire. "If we're not going to hide, then what *should* we do?"

"We do what Nick would have done." Josh stared at the flames coming from his lighter as if an idea had just occurred to him. "We stand and fight."

You failed.

It was dark when Reagan woke.

"Josh? Brooke?"

There was no answer. She was alone. Wasn't she?

You were supposed to kill him. You were supposed to kill them all.

The bloody knife lay a short distance away. Reagan remembered how she tried to kill Josh and reached out for the knife with a shaking hand.

It's not too late.

"No!" Reagan hurled the knife deeper into the cave, and it clattered to the ground somewhere in the darkness. "I'm sorry, Josh." Her voice became a whisper, and she curled into a fetal position. "It wasn't me."

Wasn't it?

She held her hands to her ears and willed the voices to stop. "I wouldn't."

We didn't force you to do anything you didn't want to.

She turned the statement over in her mind until it became a question. Had the voices forced her to do Bartholomew's bidding, or was it really her doing all along? She could hardly tell the difference anymore.

Reagan had never thought of herself as a bad person. She didn't believe in good and evil. As far as she was concerned, whatever she wanted was right. After what had happened to her mother, she kept her walls up out of a fear of showing vulnerability. She lived only for herself, but where had that taken her? She didn't have anyone left. She had pushed them all away.

Something stirred within the cave, and Reagan sat up suddenly. *What was that?* Maybe she wasn't alone after all. She couldn't decide which was worse. She paused and listened again. "Hello? Is someone there?"

Why don't you take a look and see?

Whispers called to her from the blackness. Reagan glanced toward the entrance, but the path forward was no longer visible. For the first time, it occurred to her that Bartholomew had been lying and planned to kill her with the others all along regardless of her actions. She ran her hand along the cavern wall and walked carefully through the dark in the hope she was headed in the right direction. The air felt warmer the farther she walked. Reagan spotted a light ahead and hastened her steps before coming to an abrupt halt. It wasn't moonlight she saw.

The light—red, like fire—grew brighter, illuminating the massive cavern around her. This wasn't the entrance at all. Deceived by the whispers, she had wandered deeper into the cave. Reagan froze, overcome with dread, when a voice called to her from below. This voice wasn't like the whispers. It was deep and ancient. She sensed a presence reaching out from the other side to consume her.

Reagan turned and fled back the way she came. Moonlight spilled through the cave's entrance to illuminate a towering form in her way. The voice that belonged to it was very real.

"Hello, Reagan." Wyatt held the knife she had cast aside. "I've been looking for you."

Reagan's screams echoed in the night.

Nick woke with a start.

He lay on his back on the hard earth. The ledge he had fallen from loomed above, draped in mist, impossibly far away.

I should be dead. The fall should have killed me.

He hurt everywhere, even while lying perfectly still. Every movement was pure agony. He was so tired. Every day since Grace's death had been a struggle. Nick wanted nothing more than to close his eyes and surrender to the dark, but he knew he had survived for a reason.

Nick remembered sitting alone in the back pew during her eulogy. Grace's father had found him afterward and handed him her Bible.

"She wanted you to have it," he had said simply.

Nick had no intention of reading the book, but it had belonged to Grace, so he couldn't bring himself to throw it away. He left it in a corner of his room and forgot about it as he struggled to find his way in a world without her. Then, one day, he stumbled across the book when he was feeling particularly low and opened it up. He read one page, then another, and before he knew it, he had stayed up half the night reading.

Nick was captivated by the message of repentance and forgiveness. After all the mistakes he'd made, the prospect of redemption was like a cold glass of water on a hot summer day. He'd had enough of trying to turn his life around on his own. He started going to church. Not long after that, he had been baptized. Instead of returning to school, he trained to become an EMT as a way to help others. It took a while to gather his nerve, but eventually, he called his brother in an effort to make a fresh start.

A voice called to him. "You have to get up."

For a moment, he thought he saw her in the fog. "Grace? Am I dead?" There was no answer. The disembodied voice was just that.

Nick tried pleading with her. "I'm so tired. I just want to see you again."

"You can still save them, Nick."

He tried to rise but collapsed in a heap. The pain was unbearable. "I'm sorry. I can't do this alone."

"You're not alone."

Then it dawned on him. Everything that had happened—everything he had been through—had led him to this exact moment. Grace had told him God had a plan for him, and for the first time, Nick finally understood what it was.

I can't give up now. Josh needs me.

Suddenly, he was on his feet.

He staggered forward. The effort was excruciating. It took all his strength to remain upright. Each step was torture. His shoulder was dislocated where he had fallen on it. Nick pinned himself against a tree and slammed it back into place with a scream before staring up at the ledge. Josh and the others were still out there.

He took a deep breath and started the climb.

Chapter TWENTY-TWO

5:12 A.M.

Josh stared across the farm from the forest.

Chad, just behind his shoulder, leaned forward and whispered, "What do you see?"

"Nothing. The place looks deserted."

The crows had fallen silent, and the farm was eerily quiet. He couldn't see the cultists anywhere. His eyes moved to the cornfield, where nothing stirred. No matter how abandoned the property appeared, Josh knew the evil remained.

Brooke pressed herself against him. "I have a bad feeling about this. What if they know we're coming? It could be a trap."

"She's right." Chad, still limping, shifted his weight to his good leg. "This is our last chance to turn back and wait it out until sunrise."

Josh shook his head. "The scarecrow won't stop coming after us until we're dead. We have to destroy it. It's the only way to end this."

"I thought you might say that." Chad groaned but smiled nonetheless. "Fair enough. I hope you have a plan."

"I do. We burn the cornfield and everything in it."

Chad made no attempt to hide his surprise. "Come again?"

Brooke nodded. "He's right. Setting fire to the cornfield would disrupt the ritual and keep the scarecrow away."

"I like the sound of that." Chad's bloodied lip pulled into a self-assured grin. "I'd love to see the look on that thing's face when we light it up."

"That's going to take a lot of fire." Brooke looked from Chad to Josh. "I don't think your lighter will be enough, Josh."

"The barn I crashed into earlier had plenty of gasoline cans," Chad offered. "We could use those as fuel."

"Great idea." Josh slapped him on the back. "Now we just have to figure out a way to defend ourselves in case the scarecrow comes for us first."

Brooke spoke up suddenly. "The basement the cultists kept me in was some kind of torture chamber. They had plenty of tools down there we could use as weapons."

"We'll get the weapons first and then make our way to the barn," Josh said.

"What about the crows?" Chad motioned to the crows passing over the farm.

"Follow my lead." Josh studied the birds, which flew from the cornfield and back in the same pattern every time. If he timed it just right, the group could avoid their gaze. He waited until the flock circled the farmhouse before beckoning to the others. "Now."

Once again headed for the farm, they left the trees behind and emerged into the open. Everything had come full circle. Josh's plan was audacious, which was exactly why he believed it was going to work. He was sure of it. Bartholomew would expect them to cower in fear—to continue running for their lives. That was the reason he had tried so hard to break them apart. If they stuck together, they stood a chance. Admittedly slim as it was, it was better than waiting for death. If they died, it would be fighting side-by-side. Josh would take those odds any day of the week.

"Keep low." Josh crouched under the cornstalks until the swarm passed by again. When the crows vanished from sight, he and the others crept along the cornfield's edge with the specter of the farmhouse looming in the pale moonlight. Josh scanned the area for a sign of movement, but everything was still.

Brooke grabbed his wrist. "Something's wrong. Where are all the cultists?"

She's right. It was almost too quiet. *We should have heard or seen something by now.* Josh approached the farmhouse and crossed the empty yard with a creeping sensation of dread in the pit of his stomach. He hesitated on the front steps, gazed into the cornfield, and searched for the scarecrow. *Where are you hiding?*

"Over here." Brooke lingered near a car off the gravel road. Her voice had an uncomfortable edge.

Chad knelt beside the car. "You're going to want to see this."

A cultist lay on his stomach behind the car. His robes were frayed, torn, and stained with blood. Moonlight glinted on a shotgun a few inches away.

Josh turned the hooded figure. "He's dead."

Brooke appeared to fight the urge to vomit. "What happened to him?"

The corpse had been picked clean. Only a few remnants of flesh still clung to the bloody bones. Other cultists, all dead, littered the property.

"The crows." Josh returned his attention to the corpse Brooke had discovered. "He must have tried hiding in the car, but he never made it." He picked up the gun. "We should keep moving."

Before anyone could say a word, shrieks rang out in the sky, and a shadow fell over the earth.

The crows. Josh stiffened. "They know we're here."

Wyatt, hungry for a kill, stalked across the cave. Although on the verge of losing his mind, he no longer cared. The whispers told him where he would find Reagan, just as they'd told him where he could find the one with the cross necklace. Finally, the thing in the cave was speaking to him again.

A dull roar bellowed deep inside the earth, and the ground shifted under his boots. It was waking up. He could feel its ancient power stirring to life.

The shaking stopped, and Wyatt listened for the sound of footsteps. He needed to kill Reagan before sunrise. The whispers told him so. He didn't mind that they were controlling him, or that their claws dug further into his mind the deeper he went into the cave. He had never felt so powerful. He was one with the darkness, and the darkness was one with him.

"You can't hide from me, Reagan." He dragged the bloody knife along the cavern wall and laughed—a harsh, ugly sound from his gut. He had cut off her path of escape from the cave and forced her to venture even farther inside.

When he was a boy, Wyatt's father warned him not to go near the cave. His old man wasn't superstitious by nature, but something about the cave had spooked him. Whenever Wyatt pressed him about it, his father refused to discuss the matter. Afraid of the beating he would surely receive if he disobeyed, Wyatt did as he was told and kept away from the area around the cave.

After the mine shut down, there was hardly anyone left for miles. Wyatt's older brother often told him stories about people who went missing after the entrance was discovered. Wyatt only half-believed him. Then one day, he was playing in the woods when his dog went missing. Wyatt and his brother stumbled across the cave's entrance while looking for it. Crows everywhere watched their approach from the trees around the entrance.

That was the day the thing in the cave spoke to them for the first time. It told them that they didn't have to be afraid of their father. They had killed him together later that night. His was the first body they buried in the plot, but it wasn't the last. They made a game of it, hunting campers and those who lost their way. It became a competition for them, and with each death, the voice in the cave grew stronger.

Eventually, Wyatt's brother decided he wanted to leave the land and play the game somewhere else, but Wyatt remained in the hut to hear the voice. At the moment, it told him that it needed Reagan's heart. He promised to cut it out for the Keeper. He had the rifle slung across his back in case he needed it, but it was so much more satisfying to do the deed up close and personal.

Now, where was she? Wyatt heard ragged breathing a short distance away, and his lips pulled into a cold sneer. *There.* He reached around the corner, grabbed her, and pulled her toward him.

When Reagan tried punching him in the face, Wyatt buried his false teeth in her shoulder and bit into her flesh, drawing blood. She screamed and tore free of his grip before he could slide the knife into her chest.

Wyatt straightened his back and wiped her blood from his mouth. "You taste just like I thought you would."

Clutching her bleeding shoulder, Reagan ran deeper into the cave.

Wyatt followed after her. *Keep running, girl, for all the good it will do you.*

The red light grew brighter, and the ground began to shake again.

He knew exactly where she was headed, even if she didn't.

Nick grabbed the top of the ledge, hauled himself over, and limped forward until he found the strength to walk. He shut out the pain and forced himself to keep moving forward. Eventually, he found himself in Torrent Falls, which lay utterly quiet.

There was no sign of anyone. Josh, the others, the cult, Wyatt, the scarecrow. Even the crows were gone. At least there weren't any bodies in sight. There was still a chance he could save Josh and his friends. He just had to find them first.

Nick glanced back at the shadowy barrier at the town's edge. Sunrise had inched closer, but he couldn't help wondering if Bartholomew's spell would somehow keep it at bay. *There has to be another way to lift the spell.* Nick moaned. There was only so much he could do. He had to locate the others first. Everything else would have to wait.

Careful to watch for any threats, he started on the trail that led uphill. Much to his surprise, he didn't encounter any obstacles on his way up the mountain. The mines were likewise abandoned.

Where is everyone? It was as if he were the only person left in the forest.

The moonlight glinted off a metal object near the place where Wyatt shot him hours ago, and Nick spotted Brooke's lost flashlight. He picked it up and tried switching it on. Fortunately, the light still worked.

Using the light to guide his path, Nick made his way through the woods. *The barrier would have prevented the others from going any farther east. They must have gone back the way we came.*

After a while, he came to the ruins of an old farm nestled under the mountain. Moonlight fell on a broken-down fence running along the property. The skeletal remains of a barn cast a shadow over a collapsed house.

Nick stepped on something hollow and shined his light across a wooden board. The board shifted without warning, and before he could react, it collapsed under his weight. Nick fell through a narrow opening in the ground and landed in a passage below.

He dusted himself off and again picked up the flashlight. From the look of things, he had fallen into one of the many tunnels that connected with the cave system. *How many of these things are there?*

He pointed the beam upward to expose the stone blocks of a well that had long ago run dry. There were scratch marks along the rocks, as if someone had once tried to claw their way out. The sight sent a shiver running down his back, and when Nick took an instinctive step back, something crunched underneath his shoe. Nick nearly leaped out of his skin when the flashlight uncovered a cracked skull.

More bones were scattered along the passageway. Unlike the bodies buried in the mass graves they discovered earlier, these were all skeletal remains of birds—crows, if he had to guess. There was no point in trying to climb out. He'd have to find another way back to the surface. Nick started down the tunnel and used the flashlight to illuminate the path forward. A strange red light glowed farther down the shaft.

A scream echoed from somewhere in the cave, and the hair on the back of his neck stood on end.

He wasn't alone.

Chapter TWENTY-THREE

5:33 A.M.

Josh sprinted toward the farmhouse and held the screen door open. "They saw us. We have to hurry."

As the others entered, he took one last glance at the cornfield. The cornstalks shifted in the wind, carrying the sound of whispers.

It's coming.

The screen door slammed shut behind him, and Josh followed Brooke and Chad through the parlor to a door at the hallway's end.

"Wait." Chad came to a sudden halt. "We left some cultists locked in the basement earlier."

Josh held the dead cultist's shotgun at the ready and nodded to Chad, who unlocked the door and threw it open. Josh advanced into the darkness with the gun trained ahead. A fluorescent light flickered below to reveal three figures sprawled across the cement floor in a pool of their own blood.

Josh lowered the gun and waited for the others to follow him down the stairs.

"They're all dead. Just like the others." Brooke surveyed the carnage. "How could this happen?"

The cult's demise should have been a good thing. It was one less obstacle for them to overcome. So why did Josh still feel so uneasy? "They were sacrificed. Bartholomew sacrificed his own followers."

"All?" Brooke swallowed nervously. "What kind of spell would require that?"

Josh wasn't sure, and he hoped they didn't have to find out. "Over here."

The cellar's bloodstained walls were lined with barbaric-looking tools that he guessed were probably not intended for farm use. Chad passed over a hoe in favor of a long-handled hammer. He took it from the wall and held it like a batter stepping up to the plate, and a little of his former bravado returned. Josh selected the hoe for extra protection in the event he ran out of ammunition.

"Look." Brooke, rooting around in the supply closet, held out a bag for them to see. "More flares."

"Nice." Josh noticed a box of shotgun shells on a shelf.

Without warning, the ground shook under their feet, and dust poured from the ceiling.

Brooke, startled, looked up suddenly. "What was that?"

"Let's not stick around to find out." Josh hastily scooped up the ammunition and started up the stairs. "Come on."

The group retraced their steps. Although the sky was still pitch-black, dawn was fast approaching. That was probably what made the earth shake. Bartholomew was likely growing desperate.

Josh opened the screen door and emerged onto the porch to find crows flocking above the farmhouse. His gaze fell on the cornfield, where something moved within the cornstalks; the rows parted, revealing a shadowy figure watching the house. The scarecrow stepped into the moonlight, and Josh retreated inside and slammed the door shut as it crossed the yard.

Chad tightened his grip on the hammer's handle and shot Josh a dark look. "Any more brilliant ideas, Josh?"

"We stick to the plan. That's the only way we're getting out of this alive."

"The scarecrow isn't going to stand around while we stock up on gasoline."

"I know." Josh glanced over his shoulder. "You were here before. Is there another way out?"

"Yeah." Chad shrugged. "So what? That thing will follow us no matter where we go."

"Not if I draw its attention away. Get to the barn and load the fuel into one of the vehicles. I'll give you a head start."

"No way." Brooke shook her head. "I'm not leaving you here alone. We're in this together."

Chad, peering out the window, interrupted. "I hate to rush things, but it won't be long before that thing catches up to us."

"You go then," Brooke said. "I'm staying here with Josh."

"Brooke . . ." Josh decided against trying to reason with her. Instead, he held her hand and gave it a squeeze. "You heard her, Chad."

Chad, noticing their hands entwined, chuckled. "About time you two got together." He patted Josh on the back. "Good luck, nerds." With that, he hurried away and disappeared down the hall.

Josh handed Brooke the shotgun. "Do you know how to use this thing?"

"I think so."

"Good."

The screen door swung open, and the scarecrow's shadow fell across the doorway. Josh, swinging the hoe with all his strength, charged at it, but the scarecrow caught the handle and sent him sliding along the floor. It snapped the hoe in half and tossed it aside, but before it could draw near, Brooke pointed the shotgun at its chest and pulled the trigger.

The shotgun clicked empty. Brooke tried pulling the trigger again, but nothing happened. Josh slid the box of ammunition across the floor to her, and shells spilled from her shaking fingers as she furiously tried to load it. Dragging its pitchfork behind it, the scarecrow started toward her, and her eyes widened in fear.

Josh lurched to his feet and grabbed at the scarecrow to keep it from reaching Brooke before she could reload. "Run!"

As Brooke scrambled up the staircase, the scarecrow swiped at Josh with the pitchfork, and he fell and landed on his back.

She's going the wrong way. Upstairs, there was nowhere to run. Josh pushed himself upright and rushed up the stairs. The scarecrow, waiting at the top, seized him by the throat and slammed him against the wall, cracking the wooden beams. Josh struggled to free himself, and it flung him through a doorway. He landed on the floor in the next room, where

Brooke was still attempting to load the shotgun while hiding behind the bed.

The scarecrow raised the pitchfork, but before it could finish him, Brooke leveled the shotgun and pulled the trigger. Although the blast knocked the scarecrow away, the recoil sent Brooke back through the window behind her and out onto the roof.

Josh ducked under the pitchfork and hurled himself after her. He managed to grab her hand just before she fell from the pitched roof. The shotgun slid off the roof and dropped to the ground below.

"It's okay. I've got you." He strained to support their combined weight.

Brooke, close enough to the ground to make the drop, let go of his hand and fell to a crouch in the grass. "Josh—look out!"

The scarecrow stared at him through the broken window. Before he could move, it stabbed him through the hand with the pitchfork and pinned him to the roof. Josh screamed, and the scarecrow wrenched the pitchfork free. Before it could land the killing blow, Josh grabbed the scarecrow and pulled them both over the edge of the roof.

Reagan's footsteps echoed through the cave. She glanced over her shoulder and searched for Wyatt in the shadows. He was there somewhere, waiting for the right moment to strike. She cried out when she tripped and landed on her injured shoulder. Reagan gingerly cradled the wound with blood-covered fingers. The imprints left behind by his dentures remained visible.

Reagan waited a moment longer for Wyatt to appear before picking herself up and stumbling farther along the descending path. Unlike the frigid night outside, the air was stifling. Reagan wiped the sweat from her brow and kept going. There was something else in the air—a strange scent. She tried placing the unfamiliar aroma and realized it smelled like sulfur.

She'd lost track of how far she'd traveled. How deep, exactly, did the cave extend? Soot and ash coated the ground, illuminated by the growing red light. The stones and walls were a black, igneous color. This wasn't like any cave she'd ever heard of before. It almost appeared volcanic.

The whispers and the voices grew louder until at last they were one and the same. They repeated her name over and over as she approached. Finally, she came to a place where the path ended in a massive, hollow chamber in the bowels of the earth. The air was thick with smoke. Reagan stopped short of a black ledge that dropped down into an endless abyss. There was nowhere left to go.

Then she saw the flames.

Trembling, Reagan gathered her courage and peered over the edge. "Oh my God."

A gaping, black hole swallowed everything below. The pit was full of fire, but the flames were unlike any she'd ever seen before. There were no shades of orange, or even yellow. They were pure, unadulterated red—the source of the illumination that lit the path during her descent.

More horrifying still, something was watching her from the other side. She felt its presence, ancient and powerful, fill the chamber. Its voice roared, though she could not understand its words. Dust poured from the ceiling as the cavern walls shook. She suddenly knew beyond the shadow of a doubt that the gateway the others had spoken of was real, and she was staring right into it.

Just a little farther, the whispers told her. She took another step that brought her foot dangerously close to the ledge. *You'll like it down there— trust us.*

"Reagan," a voice called out to bring her back to her senses before she could step over the ledge. When she looked up, she saw Nick, who had emerged from one of the passages that led into the chamber.

"Nick?" He was supposed to be dead, wasn't he? Did Josh tell her that, or was it the voices? Everything was so hard to remember.

"Don't do it, Reagan! Snap out of it."

Reagan blinked, and her skin crawled when she thought of what she had almost done. "Help me, please. I can't make the voices stop. I tried to kill Josh."

Nick started toward her, but before he could reach her side, another figure entered the chamber behind her.

"Nowhere left to hide, Reagan." Wyatt, wearing a malevolent grin, held up the knife and gestured to the flames. "We're in the mountain's heart."

Reagan took a step back, but the ledge was just behind her. "Stay back."

"The Keeper needs a sacrifice. Once I offer you to him, he'll be free. But don't worry—you'll see your friends soon enough. Bartholomew still needs them to complete the ritual."

He started toward her, and she braced herself for the end. At the last second, Nick came rushing at Wyatt, who noticed him a half-second too late, and the collision sent them both rolling across the ground.

Wyatt pushed himself up and gripped the knife with a snarl. "You're supposed to be dead."

They leaped at each other and met in the middle. Wyatt slashed Nick across the chest with the knife. Nick brought the flashlight up against Wyatt's head and managed to pry the knife from his hands. It went sliding across the ash-covered floor and landed at Reagan's feet.

When Wyatt put his hands around Nick's neck, Reagan rushed at him with the knife and stabbed him again and again. Wyatt roared with rage and jumped at her, and the impact carried them both over the ledge. The killer's eyes widened in surprise as his feet left the ground, and suddenly he was clutching at air, Reagan along with him.

She managed to grab hold of a rock jutting out from the ledge at the last moment. She hung there, dangling above the pit of fire. Her hand began to perspire from the heat, and she felt her grip slipping.

"Help!" She stared into the abyss below.

"Don't look down." Nick appeared at the ledge. "Give me your hand."

When Reagan started to reach for his hand, the cavern shook around her, and the voices cried out to her.

Let go, they said. *You would have killed them all. This is where you belong. It's too late for you. You can't change, not once you've embraced the darkness.*

She hesitated, and her grip slipped further.

"Don't listen to them!" Nick shouted. "You don't have to do this alone."

Reagan reached for him. His hand seized hers and he pulled her over the side. They collapsed in the soot and ash.

"Why did you help me, after everything I've done?"

Nick shook his head, as if she were missing the bigger picture. "Why do you think it's called grace?"

"I was wrong about you." Then she noticed the extent of his injuries for the first time. "You're bleeding."

"Don't worry about me. We have to get out of here and find the others."

Reagan helped Nick to his feet as the mountain continued shaking around them. "Wyatt said Bartholomew plans to complete the ritual. That means we'll probably find them at the farm." She trailed off. "There's no way we can stop it, Nick. You saw that thing. It's too powerful."

"We have to try. Think. There has to be some way to lift the spell keeping us here."

"The book. If Bartholomew's spells came from the book, maybe destroying it would break the curse." They started down the path with Reagan supporting Nick's weight. She looked back and saw a hand reaching over the ledge. "Wyatt." He had also survived the fall.

Nick followed her gaze. "Run."

The night air was cool outside the cave. When they finally reached the entrance, Nick slowed to a stop. "You go. I'll stay here and fend him off."

"Are you crazy? He has a gun."

"I know, but it's either one or both of us. At least this will give you the chance to get to the others." He stared at her with a cautious gaze. "Whatever you've done—whoever you've been—it doesn't matter. All that matters right now is telling the others about that book. I know it's tempting to try to make a run for it and hope that sunrise saves you, but I'm putting my trust in you to help save my brother. Don't let me down."

Reagan sprinted into the woods under the moonlight. "Goodbye, Nick."

Chapter TWENTY-FOUR

Josh lay on his back on the cold ground and stared up at the sky. His body hurt from the fall off the roof, but not as much as the pain in his bloodied hand where the scarecrow had pinned him to the roof. Josh moaned and rolled onto his side. The scarecrow, inches away, reached for him as the crows flocked overhead. Josh scrambled back at the sight of it, and his good hand bumped into the shotgun.

He stumbled to his feet and trained the gun on the scarecrow, which rose undaunted to tower above him. Josh took a few steps back and glanced over his shoulder, where Chad was loading gasoline canisters onto the back of a pickup truck. When the scarecrow reached for Josh, Brooke ignited a flare, which temporarily held it at bay.

"Josh!" Reagan, carrying a torch one of the fallen cultists had dropped, came sprinting across the yard.

Josh looked at her warily. "What are you doing here?"

"Your brother saved me from Wyatt."

"What?" Josh faced down the scarecrow as the flare cast its light over the yard. "You're a liar."

Reagan grabbed his wrist. "He's not dead! I was ready to let the Keeper of the Crows take me, but Nick rescued me. He wanted me to help you guys end this nightmare once and for all."

"How can we ever trust you again?"

Reagan pleaded with him with her eyes. "I'm sorry for what I did to you. I can't take it back, but I can help now. You need to listen to me. We have to destroy Bartholomew's book. It's probably the only way to break the spell."

"Almost finished. Thanks for the distraction." Chad, rolling a barrel of fuel from the barn, stopped when he caught sight of Reagan. "I thought you'd be hiding somewhere, waiting for the rest of us to die."

"Chad . . ."

"Josh told me everything. If we make it out alive, you and I need to have a long talk. I think it's time we started seeing other people."

Brooke's flare began to burn low, and the scarecrow let out a blood-curdling shriek. All across the yard, the dead cultists began to rise. Their skeletal remains, animated by an unseen force, jerked and writhed while the crows flew directly at the group from above.

"Now!" Josh shouted as the onslaught approached, and the area was flooded with light. Just as he'd planned, the others turned on the headlights of the abandoned vehicles. The group converged in the middle and stood back-to-back as the first wave of attackers hit. "Here they come!"

Josh fired the shotgun into the swarm, and birds dropped out of the sky right and left. Chad swung the long-handled hammer and sent one hooded figure after another crashing to the ground. Brooke kept lighting flares, and Reagan swung the torch through the air to scatter the flock.

The scarecrow, initially driven back by the headlights, let out an angry roar and redirected the crows with its pitchfork. They flew at the cars, killing themselves by smashing into the headlights.

"There are too many of them," Brooke shouted as more hooded figures emerged from the cornfield.

Josh pulled open the door of the truck Chad had stocked with the fuel from the barn. "Everybody inside."

Brooke slid into the passenger seat. Chad jumped onto the back and offered his hand to Reagan to pull her over the side. Josh hit the gas and ran over reanimated cultists while heading directly for the cornfield. The truck, gathering speed, plowed through the rows and flattened the cornstalks while Chad emptied cans of gasoline over the area. Reagan cast her torch into the cornfield, and a fire began to spread across the rows.

Josh glanced in his rearview mirror and saw the scarecrow running alongside them. He looked back to the path ahead in time to see crows smash through the windshield. He jerked the wheel, but it was too late. The truck overturned and slid to a stop in the dirt.

Josh, rattled by the impact, slowly undid his seatbelt and climbed from the vehicle. Where was the shotgun?

"Josh," Brooke called weakly from the passenger seat.

He shuffled over to her and helped her out of the truck. "Are you okay?"

Brooke nodded, but he could see she was pretty banged up. Reagan and Chad lay a short distance away. Although they were both moving, it was impossible to tell if they were seriously hurt.

Josh took out his lighter and headed toward the back of the truck, where the remaining canisters of gasoline spilled over the ground. "Get back, Brooke."

"What are you doing?"

"This is the only way."

Before he could act, the scarecrow stepped from behind the next row and knocked him off his feet.

"The gun!" Reagan pointed at the spot where the gun had fallen next to the truck.

Josh crawled toward it, but the scarecrow grabbed him by the ankle and pulled him away. He looked over at Chad, closest to the gun. When Chad threw himself at the shotgun, the scarecrow stabbed him through the gut. The scarecrow wrenched the pitchfork free, and blood gushed from the wound.

Chad's mouth curled up in a grin, and Josh saw that he had the shotgun in his hands.

"Looks like it's my turn to be the hero." Chad pulled the trigger.

The truck exploded, and the cornfield went up in flame.

Nick, clutching his side, limped through the woods. The pain from the knife wound was searing. He had been shot, stabbed, and thrown off a cliff. His body threatened to rebel against him, but he forced himself to keep going.

Dry leaves crunched behind him. He turned around and peered into the darkness. For a moment, he thought he saw a figure watching him from the shadows. His vision blurred, and when he blinked, the space was empty. There was no sign of Wyatt in the moonlight, but he knew the killer was out there somewhere, stalking him across the forest.

The pain was unbearable. He stumbled and nearly fell. It was almost impossible to remain upright.

I've got to keep moving. I can't give up now, not when Josh is counting on me.

The farm appeared ahead, visible from the edge of the forest, and Nick felt a flood of relief.

"It's the end of the line," a voice said from the night.

When Nick turned around, Wyatt stood across from him. The gathering wind disheveled the killer's long, thinning hair. Nick rushed at him before he could bring up the rifle, but Wyatt was too strong. He hit Nick in the face with the barrel of the gun. Nick landed on a pile of leaves and tasted blood.

Wyatt, looming over him, pointed the rifle into his face. "Listen. I can almost hear their screams over the wind."

Suddenly, the forest was awash in a fiery glow. Nick glanced over his shoulder and followed Wyatt's gaze. Fire and smoke shot into the sky from the blazing cornfield.

Josh, Nick thought.

Without warning, an explosion tore through the air. With Wyatt distracted, Nick drew on all the strength he had left and lunged for the rifle.

A single gunshot echoed across the forest.

Josh's ears were ringing. Everything was a blur. One foot after the other, he blindly pushed through the stalks. The cornfield was draped in a backdrop of fire and smoke. He looked around for his friends. Where was everyone?

Something moved behind him. He spun around, but there was nothing there.

"Josh!" Brooke called from somewhere within the rows.

"Brooke!" He followed her voice. "Where are you?"

There was no answer.

The scarecrow emerged ahead, and Josh skidded to a stop. He barely avoided the bloody pitchfork and tumbled into the next row. Josh felt its gaze following him through the corn. In the process, he nearly ran over Chad, holding his bleeding stomach as he lay on the ground.

"I think I'm just about done for, Josh." His voice was weak.

"Not yet." Josh helped him up. "It's the fourth quarter, pal."

He coughed on a lungful of smoke. Chad's wounds were bad. They needed to get him to a hospital soon. Screams sounded from deeper within the cornfield, and Josh pushed forward. He stepped past the next row and found himself inside the circle at the cornfield's heart.

Bartholomew stood at the altar, where the black book lay open. Shadows spread from his red robes as the flames glowed behind him. Josh's gaze fell on Brooke and Reagan, on the opposite side of the circle.

"You're here." Bartholomew raised his scythe, and without warning, the cornstalks came to life and bound their feet in place like ropes. As Josh struggled in vain to free himself, the scarecrow emerged and came to stand beside Bartholomew at the altar.

Above, the sky began to lighten.

"It's over. It's morning. You failed."

Bartholomew laughed, a discordant sound that sent a shiver running through Josh. "The shadows will hold the light at bay long enough for me to complete the ritual. A pity. You and your friends came close, but in the end, you were no match for . . ."

The roar of an engine drowned out his voice. Headlights burned through the shadows, and a car came crashing through the cornstalks. The vehicle ran down the scarecrow as it struck the altar and broke the stone table. The door swung open, and Nick pointed a rifle at Bartholomew and squeezed the trigger. The bullet struck the cult leader in the face and shattered half of the elk mask.

Nick cast the gun aside, limped over to Josh, and freed him from the stalks before helping the others. As the group headed to the car, stones fell to the ground at the altar, where the scarecrow began to rise.

Nick pushed him toward the car. "You have to go."

Josh shook his head. "We'll never make it—not with that barrier in place."

"I'll take care of it." Nick's gaze fell on the book.

"I'm not leaving you here alone. You're my brother."

Nick grabbed his neck and held him in an embrace while the others piled into the car. "I can't do this alone. It's up to you to get them out of here. You have to trust me."

Bartholomew's twisted form stirred, and the cult leader's fingers jerked as his body filled with life.

Josh reluctantly climbed into the driver's seat and put the car in reverse. "I'm sorry, Nick."

"Drive like hell for that barrier. Don't look back."

"Thank you."

The brothers exchanged a smile for an all-too-brief moment. Then Bartholomew rose from the ground and grabbed his scythe, and Josh turned the car around and stomped on the gas.

Nick, hunched over as flames consumed the cornfield, panted for air. The scarecrow stood between him and Bartholomew, whose face—now partially exposed—was lined with rage.

"I told you I would save them. Every one of them." Nick stared him down defiantly. "I bet your master isn't going to be too happy with you when he finds you lost to a bunch of teenagers."

"Your actions tonight mean nothing. Baal will rise again."

"Maybe—but not tonight. And if I can beat you, others can too."

"Kill him," Bartholomew commanded the scarecrow.

Nick charged forward as the scarecrow swung at him, and at the last second, he rolled under its arm and continued sprinting toward the altar.

That was as far as he got. Bartholomew impaled him with the scythe through the chest. Blood poured from Nick's mouth as the blade protruded through his back.

"Your death is at hand," the cult leader said.

Nick fell away, holding the book. "You lose."

The scarecrow started toward him, but it was too late. Nick cast the book into the flames.

The rail fence loomed just ahead. The barrier covering everything beyond it concealed the outside world in a thick fog. Josh kept his foot on the gas pedal, and the engine roared as they approached.

"Here goes nothing." He squeezed Brooke's hand, and the car smashed through the fence.

Just before they struck the barrier, sunbeams poked through the shadows, and the mist began to recede. The car burst onto the road and left the farm behind.

Josh looked over his shoulder. Chad, slumped over in the back seat, shivered and held his bloody abdomen. His skin was deathly white. Reagan, beside him, stared blankly ahead and muttered to herself. There would be scars after all they had suffered, but at least they were alive.

Brooke glanced over at him from the passenger seat. "Where are we going?"

Josh, intent on getting Chad to the hospital, stared dead ahead.

"Gray Hollow."

Epilogue

Nick leaned against the broken altar as the cornfield burned around him. The ground trembled violently, as if the caves were all collapsing inward. One by one, holes appeared in the covering of darkness.

"Finish him," Bartholomew commanded the scarecrow.

Nick didn't bother moving as it raised the pitchfork. He'd already won. The ritual had failed.

The scarecrow let out a sudden shriek, and the pitchfork fell to the ground. The scarecrow thrashed around blindly and went still, inanimate once more.

Bartholomew stepped forward, clutching the scythe, but a brilliant light broke through the remains of the barrier and stopped him dead in his tracks. The cult leader removed the elk skull and dropped it to the ground. Then he grabbed the scarecrow and retreated into the burning rows.

Nick lay there and watched the sunrise. He'd never seen anything so beautiful in all his life. The pain was almost gone. He could hardly feel a thing. His eyes began to grow heavy. He was so tired.

A white light appeared ahead, and a figure approached him through the rows.

"You did it. I always knew you could."

"Grace?" he mumbled.

She looked almost the same as he remembered, except healthy and strong. "It's time to go home, Nick."

As the sun filled the sky, Nick smiled and reached for her hand.

Acknowledgments

I'm always surprised at the heart of these *Keeper* books. Somehow, what starts as a story about an evil scarecrow always finds a way to become something more than I intended. The story grows and changes with the characters in ways I don't always anticipate.

In some aspects, *Vengeance* is more of a spiritual sequel to another of my books—*A Sound in the Dark*—than a direct sequel to *The Whispers of the Crows*. Both *Vengeance* and *Sound* follow a group of campers trying to survive a night in the woods. Each pits them against murderous forces that test their sanity and will to survive.

Everybody's supposed to die in a book like this. That's how the formula works. In a horror story—especially where a group of teenage campers is concerned—usually there's only one person who makes it out at the end. That's not far from the direction I originally planned to take with *Vengeance*. After all, how is a group of five campers supposed to survive a cult, a murder of vengeful crows, a psychopath, *and* a supernatural scarecrow? It should have been a bloodbath.

But these weren't just any teenagers. They were all broken in their own ways. They all had to deal with suffering and pain and learn to grow. Because of that, they weren't the easy pickings the cult imagined them to be. So, instead, the formula was inverted. One main character managed to find a way to rescue everyone and, despite the overwhelming odds against them, the others made it out alive. In the end, Nick kept his promise to his brother. Now, he can finally rest.

From the start, I've wanted every book in this series to stand on its own. Although the stories all connect, I've tried to tell a different kind of horror story with each book. *Keeper* was a creepy supernatural mystery in a town with hidden secrets. *Whispers* was about a boy finding his courage. *Vengeance* followed a group of campers as they tried to survive a night of terror.

I'm excited to tell the end of the story.

There are many people I would like to acknowledge for their help with this book. First off, my parents, Robert and Pam Romines. My mother, the first person to read this book, provided me with some invaluable early feedback that shaped the direction of my initial revision. I would like to acknowledge Jennifer Cappello, who edited the book and the others in the series, as well as the Sunbury Press production team that put this book together. I also want to thank my proofreader, Margaret Dean. Additionally, I want to thank the team at Damonza for providing a beautiful cover for another of my books.

And finally, thank *you* for reading! If you enjoyed the story, I encourage you to let me know by leaving a review on Amazon or Goodreads. If you are interested in reading more by me, be sure to check my Amazon author page for a list of all my books currently available for purchase. And, of course, feel free to contact me if you wish to discuss this story or anything else.

Thanks again,
Kyle

About the Author

KYLE ALEXANDER ROMINES is a teller of tales from the hills of Kentucky. He enjoys good reads, thunderstorms, and anything edible. His writing interests include fantasy, science fiction, horror, and western.

Kyle's debut horror novel, *The Keeper of the Crows*, appeared on the Preliminary Ballot of the 2015 Bram Stoker Awards in the category of Superior Achievement in a First Novel. He obtained his M.D. from the University of Louisville School of Medicine.

You can contact Kyle at thekylealexander@hotmail.com. You can also subscribe to his author newsletter to receive email updates and a FREE electronic copy of his science fiction novella, *The Chrononaut*, at http://eepurl.com/bsvhYP.